AN ELEMENTARY COURSE OF
FOOD CHEMISTRY

MAXWELL PRESS

AN ELEMENTARY COURSE OF FOOD CHEMISTRY

Zella P. Egdahl, B.S., M.S.

MAXWELL PRESS

Chennai   Trichy   New Delhi

MAXWELL PRESS

The edition has been published in india by arrangement with Carson Books, UK

ISBN 978-81-8094-311-9   **Maxwell Press**

All rights reserved   No. 44, Nallathambi Street,
Printed and bound in India   Triplicane, Chennai 600 005

MJP 979   © Publishers, 2023

Publisher :   **C. Janarthanan**

Publisher's Note

The legacy of a country is in its varied cultural heritage, historical literature, developments in the field of economy and science. The top nations in the world are competing in the field of science, economy and literature. This vast legacy has to be conserved and documented so that it can be bestowed to the future generation. The knowledge of this legacy is slowly getting perished in the present generation due to lack of documentation.

Keeping this in mind, the concern with retrospective acquiring of rare books has been accented recently by the burgeoning reprint industry. Maxwell Press is gratified to retrieve the rare collections with a view to bring back those books that were landmarks in their time.

In this effort, a series of rare books would be republished under the banner, "Maxwell Press". The books in the reprint series have been carefully selected for their contemporary usefulness as well as their historical importance within the intellectual. We reconstruct the book with slight enhancements made for better presentation, without affecting the contents of the original edition.

Most of the works selected for republishing covers a huge range of subjects, from history to anthropology. We believe this reprint edition will be a service to the numerous researchers and practitioners active in this fascinating field. We allow readers to experience the wonder of peering into a scholarly work of the highest order and seminal significance.

Maxwell Press

PREFACE

In the preparation of this manual the aim has been to organize a practical course of food chemistry for secondary schools, and, also, to include in one book material from widely different sources. The exercises have been selected from books of organic, physiological, industrial, and sanitary chemistry, with the modifications necessary for secondary school work.

The course requires an elementary knowledge of general chemistry. It is intended primarily for students of domestic science who desire a knowledge of food chemistry applicable to the chemical problems involved in cookery and household science.

It is advisable to use the simplest possible apparatus in the experimental work. Much needless waste of time can be saved by the elimination of complex apparatus. Most of the exercises can be completed in an ordinary laboratory period of an hour and a half.

Since organic chemistry is not a prerequisite of the course it is necessary to introduce some preliminary work in this subject before proceeding with the chemistry of the food-stuffs. A few experiments on the hydrocarbons and their derivatives precede the study of the fats, carbohydrates, and proteins. The subject matter is ar-ranged in accordance with the presentation in most books of organic chemistry. Special reference reading in Perkin and Kipping's Organic Chemistry, (London, 1907) and in Noyes' Organic Chemistry, (N. Y., 1903) is indicated at the beginning of each experiment. Any text book of organic chemistry may be used in connection with class room instruction. In the bibliography the

books which are of most importance for general reference are marked with an asterisk.

I wish to acknowledge my indebtness to Mr. T.
R. Moyle, of Stout Institute, for many valuable sugges-
tions and also for help in the reading of the proof.

Zella P. Egdahl.

Menomonie, Wisconsin, January, 1913.

CONTENTS

CHAPTER I

Composition of Organic Substances

Organic chemistry has developed from the study of products obtained from plant and animal substances. **At** the close of the 18th century **Lavoisier,** a French chemist, demonstrated that, when the organic products of vegetable and animal organisms are burned, carbon dioxide and water are always formed. Lavoisier showed also that the component elements of these bodies are generally **carbon, hydrogen,** and **oxygen,** and frequently **nitrogen.** It was believed for a long time that organic substances could not be formed synthetically from the elements, but could be formed only as a result of vital processes. This conception was disproved by **Woehler** who succeeded in preparing urea from ammonium cyanate in 1828. Since then most of the organic compounds have been artificially prepared. **Organic compounds all contain carbon so that organic chemistry is now defined as the study of the compounds of carbon.** Carbon forms an exceedingly large number of compounds, over 60,000 in all, so that a study of these must necessarily be made a separate branch of chemistry. The simplest compounds of carbon are the compounds of carbon with hydrogen, called hydrocarbons. Besides these we have compounds of carbon, hydrogen and oxygen, and many which contain nitrogen in addition. Sulphur and phosphorus also enter into the composition of many organic compounds. It is possible to introduce, artificially, almost all of the elements, both metals and non-metals, as constituents of carbon compounds. The number of known carbon compounds is therefore very great.

Experiment No. 1.—Composition of Organic Compounds

Reading—P. & K., p. 3.
         N., pp. 1-4.

Apparatus.—4 test-tubes, beaker (100cc.), crucible, ring-stand, burner.

Material.—Cane sugar, egg yolk, soda-lime, sodium carbonate, potassium nitrate, concentrated nitric acid, ammonium molybdate solution, barium chloride solution.

Tests.

1.—Place two grams of sugar in a test-tube and heat until vapors are given off. Notice the formation of moisture on the sides of the test-tube. Test the **inflammability** of the vapors by holding a flame to the mouth of the test-tube. Continue the heating until vapors are no longer evolved. What is left in the test-tube? Break the tube and examine the residue. Sugar is composed of which elements?

2.—Allow half of an egg yolk to dry between filter paper, or, better, dry on a watch glass in the warming oven. Mix a small amount of the dry egg yolk with an excess of soda-lime, transfer to a test-tube and heat. Test the reaction of the vapors to moist litmus paper. Do the fumes smell of ammonia gas? Hold a rod moistened in hydrochloric acid to the mouth of the test-tube. What occurs? Do all organic compounds contain nitrogen.

3.—Prepare a fusion mixture by mixing equal amounts of powdered potassium nitrate and sodium carbonate. To a piece of the dry egg yolk the size of a pea add an equal amount of the fusion mixture and fuse in a crucible on a clay triangle over the free flame. When mixture is well fused, (the substance melts and then solidifies), allow to cool. Divide the fused mass into two portions and reserve one portion for 4. Dissolve the other portion in 5 cc. of dilute nitric acid, filter, and add 5 cc. of ammonium molybdate to the filtrate. The formation of a fine yellow precipitate, especially on warming, indicates the presence of phosphates. By treatment with the fusion mixture the phosphorus in the egg yolk has been converted into a phosphate compound.

4.—Dissolve the remainder of the fused mass in 5 cc. of dilute hydrochloric acid, filter into a test-tube and add a few drops of barium chloride solution. The formation of a white precipitate indicates the presence of sulphates. The fusion mixture oxidizes the sulphur in the egg yolk to a sulphate compound.

Place a small amount of egg yolk on a bright silver coin. Moisten and allow to stand for a few minutes. What is the result? What causes the tarnishing of silver?

CHAPTER II

Hydrocarbons

Classification of Hydrocarbons—Richter, Organic Chemistry, p. 78.

I. **Fatty Bodies:** Aliphatic compounds, chain-like carbon compounds, methane series.

II. **Carbocyclic Compounds:** Aromatic compounds, carbon ring compounds, benzene series.

III. **Heterocyclic Compounds:** Mixed ring compounds.

I. **Fatty Bodies.**

A. **Saturated Hydrocarbons,** Paraffins.
$C_n H_{2} {}_2$

Lower Members of Paraffin Series With all Known Isomerides.

Paraffin	Boiling Point
1. Methane, CH_4	$-160°$
2. Ethane, C_2H_6	$-93°$
3. Propane, C_3H_8	$-45°$
4. Butanes, C_4H_{10}	
Normal	$+1°$
Iso-butane	$-17°$
5. Pentanes, C_5H_{12}	
Normal	$38°$
Dimethyl-ethyl methane	$30°$
Tetra-methyl methane	$10°$
6. Hexanes, C_6H_{14}	
Normal hexane	$71°$
Methyl-diethyl methane	$64°$
Dimethyl-propyl methane	$62°$
Di-iso propyl	$58°$
Trimethyl-ethyl methane	$43°$

Higher Members of the Known Normal Hydrocarbons.

	Melting Point	Boiling Point	Sp. Gr.
7. Heptane, C_7H_{16}		98.4°	0.7006 (0°)
8. Octane, C_8H_{18}		125.5°	0.7188 (0°)
9. Nonane, C_9H_{20}	—51°	149.5°	0.7330 (0°)
10. Decane, $C_{10}H_{22}$	—32°	173°	0.7456 (0°)
11. Undecane, $C_{11}H_{24}$	—26.5°	194.5°	0.7745 (m. p.)
12. Dodecane, $C_{12}H_{26}$	—12°	214°	0.773 (m. p.)
13. Tridecane, $C_{13}H_{28}$	—6.2°	234°	0.775 (m. p.)
14. Tetradecane, $C_{14}H_{30}$	5.5°	252.5°	0.775 (m. p.)
15. Pentadecane, $C_{15}H_{32}$	10°	270.5°	0.775 (m. p.)
16. Hexadecane, $C_{16}H_{34}$	18°	287.5°	0.775 (m. p.)
17. Heptadecane, $C_{17}H_{36}$	22.5°	303°	0.776 (m. p.)
18. Octadecane, $C_{18}H_{33}$	28°	317°	0.776 (m. p.)
19. Nonadecane, $C_{19}H_{40}$	32°	330°	0.777 (m. p.)
20. Eicosane, $C_{20}H_{42}$	36.7°	205° (15mm. pr.)	0.777 (m. p.)
21. Heneicosane, $C_{21}H_{44}$	40.4°	215° (15mm. pr.)	0.778 (m. p.)
22. Docosane, $C_{22}H_{46}$	44.4°	224.5° (15mm. pr.)	0.778 (m. p.)
23. Tricosane, $C_{23}H_{48}$	47.7°	234° (15mm. pr.)	0.778 (m. p.)
24. Tetracosane, $C_{24}H_{50}$	51.5°	243° (15mm. pr.)	0.778 (m. p.)

	Melting Point	Boiling Point	Sp. Gr.
27. Heptacosane, $C_{27}H_{56}$	59.5°	270°(15mm. pr.)	0.779 (m. p.)
31. Hentriacontane, $C_{31}H_{64}$	68.1°	302°(15mm. pr.)	0.780 (m. p.)
32. Dotriacontane, $C_{32}H_{66}$	70°	310°(15mm. pr.)	0.781 (m. p.)
35. Pentatriacontane, $C_{35}H_{72}$	74.7°	331°(15mm. pr.)	0.781 (m. p.)
60. Dimyricyl, $C_{60}H_{122}$	102°		

B. Unsaturated Hydrocarbons.
   1. Olefines.
   2. Acetylenes.

Paraffins

Physical Properties of the Paraffins. The lower members of the paraffins up to butane are gases, the intermediate members are colorless liquids, and the higher members beginning with hexadecane, $C_{16}H_{34}$, are solids. The paraffins are insoluble in water, but the lower and intermediate compounds dissolve readily in alcohol and in ether. The solubility decreases with the increase in molcular weight. Dimyricyl, $C_{60}H_{122}$ is quite insoluble. It will be seen from the tables that the boiling point increases with the increase in molecular weight.

Chemical Properties. The paraffins are chain-like compounds. The structural formulae assigned to some of the lower members are as follows:

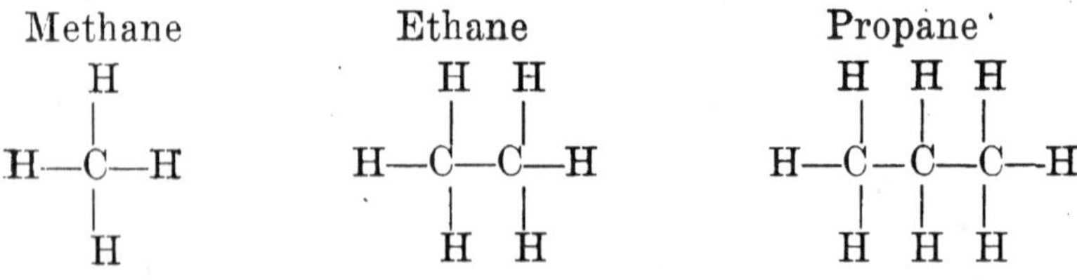

Normal butane Isobutane, (trimethyl methane)

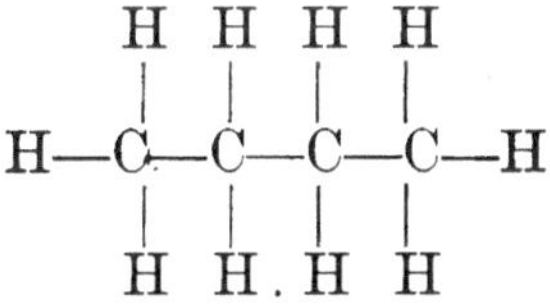

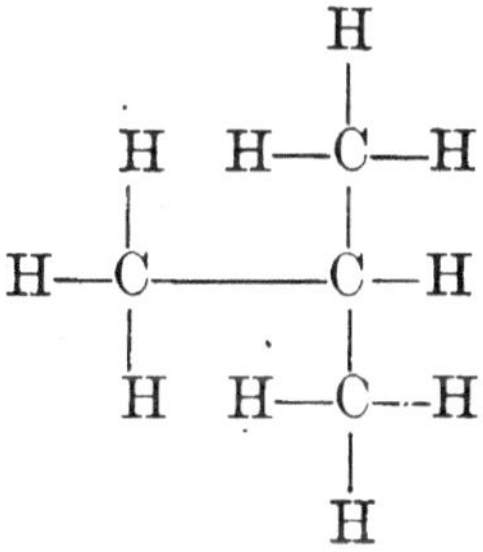

The paraffins form a homologous series of hydrocarbons. Each member differs from the preceeding member by a constant difference of CH_2. Beginning with butane they occur in isomeric forms. Isomers are compounds which have the same molecular formula but which differ in constitution. Compare the structural formulae of butane and isobutane.

The paraffins are very stable, saturated compounds. When heated they burn forming carbon dioxide and water. The chief reactions of the paraffins are substitution reactions. It is possible by chemical methods to substitute for the hydrogen atoms in the compounds other univalent elements or groups. One or more of the hydrogen atoms may be so substituted. It is possible to replace the hydrogen by a halogen, a hydroxyl group, an amido group, a nitro group and so forth. The most important substitution products of the paraffins are the mono-substitution products, i. e., the compounds in which one hydrogen has been replaced. These mono-substitution products are called alkyl compounds. The hydrocarbon radical in these compounds is called the alkyl radical and is represented by R in the general formulae of the compounds.

Paraffin	Alkyl radical	**A**lkyl chloride
C_nH_{2n+2}	C_nH_{2n-1} (R)	RCl
Ethane C_2H_6	Ethyl radical C_2H_5	Ethyl chloride C_2H_5Cl
Propane C_3H_8	Propyl radical C_3H_7	Propyl chloride C_3H_7Cl

Below is a list of the chief derivatives of the paraffins:

Alcohols, ROH
Ethers, ROR
Aldehydes, RCHO
Ketones, RCOR
Acids, RCOOH
Esters, RCOOR

The relation between some of these compounds may be seen by the following table:

Paraffin	Alcohol	**A**ldehyde	Acid
methane CH_4	methyl alcohol CH_3OH	formaldehyde $HCHO$	formic acid $HCOOH$
ethane C_2H_6	ethyl alcohol C_2H_5OH	acetaldehyde CH_3CHO	acetic acid CH_3COOH
propane C_3H_8	propyl alcohol C_3H_7OH	propaldehyde C_2H_5CHO	propionic acid C_2H_5COOH

Methane. Methane, CH_4, or marsh gas, is the first member of the paraffin series of hydrocarbons. It is formed by the decay of vegetable matter and is liberated in swamps and in mines. When mixed with air methane forms an explosive mixture, the deadly fire-damp of coal mines. Methane with other gaseous hydrocarbons occurs in natural gas and in illuminating gas. American petroleum is rich in the paraffin hydrocarbons. Methane may be obtained from petroleum by fractional distillation but it is very difficult to isolate it completely from the other hydrocarbons. In the laboratory methane is made by heating a mixture of sodium acetate and soda lime. The reaction is between the acetate and the sodium hydroxide. The lime is used to prevent corrosion of the glass vessel through the action of the molten sodium hydroxide.

$$CH_3COONa + NaOH \rightarrow Na_2CO_3 + CH_4$$

Experiment No. 2.—Methane.

Reading—P. & K. p. 53.

N. p. 58.

Apparatus. Round bottom flask (250cc.), cork, delivery tube, iron stand fitted with iron ring and clamp, 4 small wide mouth bottles (6 oz.), dish of water, Bunsen burner, wire gauze.

Material. Dehydrated sodium acetate, sodium hydroxide, quick lime.

Preparation. Fit a round bottom flask with cork and delivery tube; thoroughly mix 10g of dehydrated sodium acetate, 10g. of powdered sodium hydroxide, and 15g. of quick-lime and add to flask. Heat flask carefully but strongly over a wire gauze. Collect three bottles of the gas by displacement of water.

Tests.

1.—Apply a lighted splint to the gas in the first bottle. Describe the flame.

2.—Invert a bottle of air over the second bottle of gas. In a few seconds test both bottles with a lighted splint. Is methane lighter or heavier than air?

3.—Has methane any color or odor?

Acetylene. Acetylene, C_2H_2, is an unsaturated hydrocarbon. It can be prepared directly from its elements. When an electric spark is passed between carbon points in an atmosphere of hydrogen, acetylene is formed.

$$2C + H_2 \rightarrow C_2H_2$$

Acetylene is made commercially by the action of water upon calcium carbide.

$$CaC_2 + 2H_2O \rightarrow Ca(OH)_2 + C_2H_2$$

Acetylene when pure has a pleasant, ethereal odor and can be liquified at $+1°$ under a pressure of 48 atmospheres. Acetylene burns with a smoky flame and when mixed with air forms an explosive mixture. Specially constructed burners have been devised in which acetylene can be burned without smoking. Under these conditions the acetylene flame is very brilliant.

Acetylene like the other members of the unsaturated hydrocarbons is very active. It combines directly with the halogens forming ethylene and ethane halides. It also unites with hydrogen forming ethylene and ethane. Acetylene reacts with the metals to form metallic acetylides some of which are very explosive. For this reason it is unsafe to store acetylene gas in metallic holders. Acetylene polymerizes at red heat and forms benzene. Three molecules unite to form one molecule of benzene.

$$3C_2H_2 \rightarrow C_6H_6$$

Experiment No. 3.—Acetylene

Reading—P. & K. p. 81.

           N. p. 87.

Apparatus. 3 wide mouth bottles, basin of water.

Material. Calcium carbide, bromine water.

Preparation. Drop a small lump of calcium carbide into a basin of water and collect three bottles of the gas by displacement of water.

Tests.

1.—Describe the physical properties of the gas.

2.—Apply a lighted splint to the gas in one of the bottles. Describe the flame.

3.—Add a few drops of bromine water to the third bottle of gas. What is formed? Notice the odor.

Illuminating Gas. When bituminous coal is heated to a high temperature in the absence of air it is decomposed into a number of products one of which is illuminating gas. The process is known as destructive distillation. The diagram illustrates the products obtained by the destructive distillation of Newcastle coal.

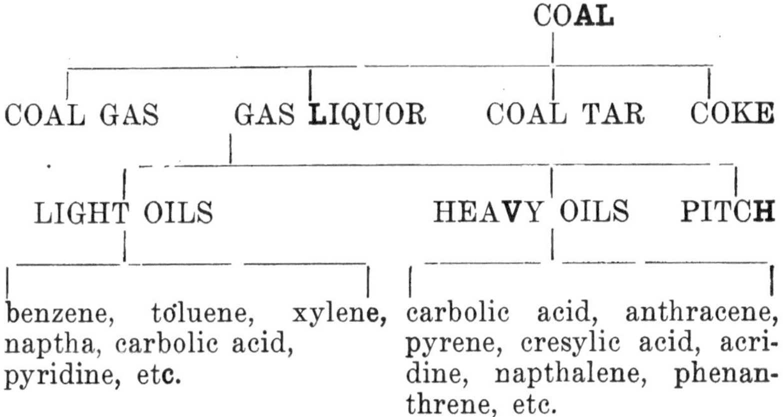

Illuminating gas is a mixture of methane, some of the heavier hydrocarbons, carbonic oxide, hydroyen, oxygen, and carbon dioxide.

Experiment No. 4.—Illuminating gas

Apparatus. Hard glass test-tube, one hole stopper, delivery tube, pan, wide mouth bottle, clamp, ringstand, burner.

Material. Soft coal.

Preparation. Fill a hard glass test-tube one third full of soft coal, fit with a cork and delivery tube; clamp the test-tube in a horizontal position and heat, gently at first, and then quite strongly. Collect gas by displacement of water.

Tests.

1.—What are the physical properties of the gas? Is the gas pure?

2.—Hold a lighted splint to the mouth of a bottle of the gas.

3.—Collect a bottle of gas from the gas jet and compare with the coal gas which you have prepared.

Benzene. Benzene is the first member of the carbocyclic or ring compounds. Carbocyclic means that carbon atoms alone form the ring. When some other element besides carbon enters into the ring the compound is designated as heterocyclic. The structural formula which Kekule has assigned to benzene is given below:

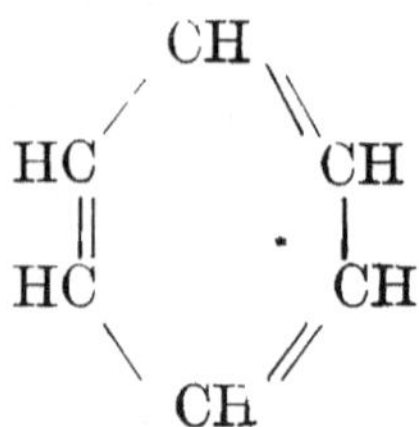

Other formulae have been proposed but in every case the ring formation is represented. The cyclic compounds are compounds in which the carbon atoms are joined to each other in such a way as to form a ring of carbons. It can easily be seen that these compounds differ quite materially from the aliphatic or open chain compounds. The benzene hydrocarbons are sometimes called the aromatic hydrocarbons.

Benzene is obtained from coal tar by distillation. A number of other hydrocarbons of this series are obtained in the same way. The principal compounds are named in the table below:

Benzene series of hydrocarbons, C_nH_{2n-6}

Benzene	C_6H_6
Toluene	C_7H_8
Xylene	C_8H_{10}
Mesitylene Pseudocumene	C_9H_{12}
Durene Cymene	$C_{10}H_{14}$
Hexa-methyl benzene	$C_{12}H_{18}$

In the laboratory benzene is made by heating benzoic acid or calcium benzoate with soda-lime. Benzene is manufactured on a large scale for use in the preparation of the dye-stuffs.

Experiment No. 5.—Benzene. Nitro-benzene

Reading—P. & K. p. 305.
> N. p. 93 p. 107.

Apparatus. Large test-tube, stopper, delivery tube, ring-stand, clamp, condenser tube, Bunsen burner.

Material. Benzoic acid, quick lime, conc. nitric acid, conc. sulphuric acid.

Preparation. Mix 8 grams of benzoic acid with an equal weight of quick lime and place in a large, dry test-tube fitted with a one hole stopper. Clamp the test-tube in a horizontal position and connect with a dry condenser tube. Heat the test-tube gently at first and then quite strongly. Continue heating until several cc. of distillate collect in the receiver.

$$C_6H_5COOH + CaO \rightarrow C_6H_6 + CaCO_3$$

Tests.

1.—What are the physical properties of benzene?

2.—Pour a few drops of the distillate into a small evaporating dish of water. Is the distillate heavier or lighter than water. Apply a lighted splint to the surface of the water.

3. **Nitrobenzene.**—Mix 2 cc. of concentrated nitric acid with the same amount of concentrated sulphuric acid in a test-tube and add gradually the remainder of the distillate, keeping the mixture at a temperature under 50°; allow the mixture to stand for a few minutes and then pour into a beaker of water. The nitrobenzene separates out as a heavy yellow oil which has the odor of almonds.

Experiment No. 6.—Fractional Distillation of Benzole

Reading—P. & K. pp. 10-12.
> N. p. 13.

Apparatus. Distilling flask, condenser and condenser

clamps, ring-stand, thermometer, 6 Erlenmeyer flasks (100cc.), wire gauze, burner.

Material. Commercial benzole, ("90 percent benzole.")

Distillation of Benzole. Commercial benzole consists of a mixture of about 70 per cent benzene and 24 per cent tolulene with some other impurities. The boiling point of benzene is 81°, and of toulene 111°. Benzole being a mixture will boil at some temperature lying between the boiling points of its constituents. It is possible by fractional distillation to separate the mixture into its constituents.

Place 100cc. of benzole in a distilling flask fitted with stopper and thermometer the bulb of which is level with the side tube of the flask. Connect the flask with the distilling apparatus. Have ready 6 small dry flasks in which to collect the different portions of the distillate. Label the flasks as follows: No. 1. Under 80°, No. 2. 80-85°, No. 3. 85-90°, No. 4. 90-95°, No. 5. 95-100°, No. 6. Over 100°.

Carefully heat the benzole and when it begins to boil, collect in flask No. I. the fraction which comes over under 80°, then change the receiver and collect in the second flask the fraction which distills over between 80 and 85°. Continue the distillation until all six fractions have been collected. Measure the amount of each fractional distillate and record the amounts in your note book. When the temperature reaches 110°, cease the distillation. Pour the residue in the distilling flask into another vessel; add the first fraction, i. e., that which distilled over under 80°, to the distilling flask and again collect the fraction under 80° in flask No. I. As soon as the temperature reaches 80°, remove flame and add the second fraction to the distilling flask. Again distill, collecting the distillate which comes over under 80° in flask No. 1., and that which comes over between 80° and 85° in flask No. 2. As soon as the temperature reaches 85°, remove the flame and add the third fraction. In the same way add the fourth fraction at 90°, the fifth at 95°, and

so on until all the six fractions have been refractionated
Again measure the fractional distillates. Redistill all
the fractions again. This time it will be seen that there
is a definite separation of the distillate into two liquids,
one having a boiling point around 82°, and the other
boiling near 110°. Measure the amount of your final
fractions.

CHAPTER III.

Alcohols

Monohydric Alcohols. The monohydric alcohols are alcohols containing one hydroxyl group. They are represented by the general formula ROH in which R stands for the hydrocarbon radical. They may be regarded as derivatives of the hydrocarbons in which one hydrogen has been replaced by the hydroxyl group.

Methane—CH_4, Methyl alcohol—CH_3OH.
Ethane—C_2H_6, Ethyl alcohol—C_2H_5OH.
Propane—C_3H_8, Propyl alcohol—C_3H_7OH.

Only one methyl and one ethyl alcohol are known. There are two isomeric propyl alcohols, four butyl alcohols and, of the higher alcohols, many isomerides can be obtained. The difference between the isomeric alcohols is illustrated by the structural formulae of the propyl and butyl alcohols.

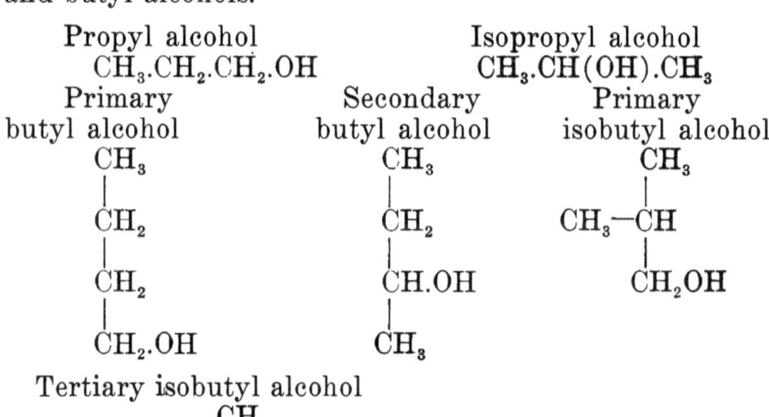

Alcohols which have the formula $R-CH_2 OH$ are classed as primary alcohols. Secondary alcohols correspond to the general formula R_2CHOH. Tertiary alcohols have the formula R_3COH. **A** primary alcohol on oxidation yields an aldehyde, and on further oxidation an acid is formed. The acid contains **as** many carbon atoms as the alcohol from which it is derived. Secondary alcohols on oxidation yield ketones. On oxidation ketones yield acids of less number of carbon atoms than the parent molecule. **Tertiary** alcohols break down on oxidation into simpler compounds. The oxidation products of the alcohols are very important since they serve to indicate the nature of **the** alcohol, that is, whether the alcohol is a primary, secondary, or tertiary compound.

Primary
alcohol   Aldehyde
$$R-CH_2OH+O \rightarrow R-CHO+H_2O$$
Aldehyde   Acid
$$R-CHO+O \rightarrow R-COOH$$
Secondary
alcohol   Ketone
$$R_2CHOH+O \rightarrow R_2CO+H_2O$$

Polyhydric Alcohols. Polyhydric alcohols are alcohols containing two or more hydroxyl groups. Glycerine, the alcohol obtained from fats, is one of the most important of the polyhydric alcohols. Glycerine is a trihydric alcohol and has the formula $C_3H_5(OH)_3$.

Ethyl Alcohol, C_2H_5OH. Ethyl alcohol, (grain alcohol), and methyl alcohol, (wood alcohol), are the alcohols most commonly used. Methyl alcohol is prepared from the products of the destructive distillation of wood. Ethyl alcohol is prepared commercially by the fermentation of solutions containing sugar. The sugar solutions are obtained from the molasses left after the removal of crystallizable sugars, or from solutions prepared from starchy substances. The latter products are generally made from corn or potatoes.

The fermentation of the sugar is caused by chemical ferments, or enzymes, secreted by yeast. The action of enzymes is not definitely known. They are supposed to act as catalytic agents. Yeast causes the fermentation of solutions of cane sugar as well as solutions of simpler sugars, i. e. glucose. If cane sugar is used it is first converted into simpler sugars through the action of an enzyme in yeast called invertase. The simple sugars are then decomposed into alcohol and carbon dioxide through the action of another enzyme, zymase.

$$\underset{\text{Cane sugar}}{C_{12}H_{22}O_{11}} + H_2O \longrightarrow \underset{\text{invertase glucose}}{C_6H_{12}O_6} + \underset{\text{fructose}}{C_6H_{12}O_6}$$

$$\underset{C_6H_{12}O_6}{} \xrightarrow{\text{zymase}} \underset{\text{Alcohol}}{2C_2H_5OH} + \underset{\text{carbon dioxide}}{2CO_2}$$

Experiment No. 7.—Alcohol

Reading—P. & K. pp. 89-103.
  N. pp. 124-134

Apparatus. Flask (500cc.), stopper, delivery tube, wide mouth bottle, condenser, Erlenmeyer flasks (75cc). evaporating dish, test-tube, thermometer.

Material. Molasses, compressed yeast cake, lime water, kerosene, iodine crystals, potassium carbonate solution.

Preparation. In a 500cc. flask place 200cc. of water and 25cc. of molasses. Mix well and add ¼ of a cake of compressed yeast which has previously been mixed with a little luke warm water (i. e. water at 37°). Stopper flask with a stopper fitted with a delivery tube which dips beneath the surface of some lime water in a wide mouth bottle. This bottle should not be stoppered, but the surface of the lime water should be covered with a layer of kerosene to exclude the air. Set the apparatus in a warm place for 24 hours. At the end of that time, if fermentation has been vigorous, (this can be judged by **the** cloudiness of the lime water), strain the contents of the flask through muslin. Place the strained liquid in a distilling flask fitted with a thermometer and connect with condenser. Heat the flask carefully until the liquid boils; then regulate the heat so as to keep the liquid boiling gently. Distill about 50cc. of distillate. Place distillate in a clean, dry distilling flask, fitted with thermometer, add a few lumps of quick lime and re-distill. Watch the temperature and cease the distillation as soon as the temperature rises above 90°. **A** few cc. of impure alcohol are obtained by this method.

Tests.

1.—Place 2cc. of the alcohol in an evaporating dish and ignite.

2.—Place 1cc. of the alcohol in a test-tube, add a small crystal of iodine and then add 1cc. of potassium carbonate solution. Warm gently and observe odor and precipitate. Alcohol is converted into iodoform by this method, and, if enough alcohol is present, a yellow precipitate of iodoform will separate out. Even with traces of alcohol, however, the odor of iodoform is quite distinct.

Questions.

1.—What was the milky precipitate in the flask of lime water?

2.—**H**ow is alcohol prepared commercially?

3.—How can alcohol be separated from water?

CHAPTER IV

Ethers

Ethers are alkyl derivatives of the alcohols. They have the general formula ROR.

Methyl Ether. Methyl ether, CH_3OCH_3, is prepared by heating methyl alcohol with sulphuric acid. It is a gas having a pleasant, ethereal odor. It can be liquified at $-23°$.

Ethyl Ether. Ethyl ether or ether, $C_2H_5OC_2H_5$, is the most important of the ethers. It has been known for a very long time. It was described in the 16th century by a German physician. Ether is prepared from ethyl alcohol and sulphuric acid. It is a pleasant-smelling colorless liquid boiling at 35°. It is volatile and **highly inflammable.** Ether is used as a solvent and as an anesthetic.

Experiment No. 8—Ether

Reading—P. & K. pp. 111-118.

N. pp. 164-168.

Apparatus. Test-tube, Bunsen burner.

Material. Concentrated sulphuric acid, alcohol.

Test.

Carefully add 5cc. of conc. sulphuric acid to a test-tube containing 5cc. of alcohol. Warm gently until the liquid appears to boil. Determine the odor of the product in the test-tube. Ether is formed by the interaction of the alcohol and acid. Ethyl hydrogen sulphate is first formed and this reacts with more alcohol to form ether. The process is continuous.

$$C_2H_5OH + H_2SO_4 \rightarrow C_2H_5HSO_4 + H_2O$$
$$C_2H_5HSO_4 + C_2H_5OH \rightarrow C_2H_5OC_2H_5 + H_2SO_4$$

CHAPTER V

Aldehydes and Ketones

Aldehydes. The aldehydes are intermediate products formed by the oxidation of primary alcohols. When the alcohols are completely oxidized acids are formed. It is possible, however, by proper precautions, to obtain products intermediate between the alcohols and acids. These products are called **aldehydes,** from **alcohol dehydrogenatum,** since they may be regarded as alcohols from which hydrogen has been removed.

Formaldehyde. Formaldehyde is the aldehyde most commonly used. It is probably the first product formed in the synthesis of carbohydrates in vegetable cells. It is prepared by passing vaporized methyl alcohol, mixed with air, over heated platinised asbestos. $CH_3 . OH + O \rightarrow H . CHO + H_2O$. Special lamps have been constructed for the production of the gas. Formaldehyde is a gas at ordinary temperatures. It can easily be condensed to a liquid having a boiling point of $-21°$. Formaldehyde dissolves readily in water. **Formalin** is a commercial solution of formaldehyde containing about 40 per cent of the gas. An aqueous solution of formalin reduces metallic hydroxides, forming metallic oxides. With ammoniacal silver nitrate solution, metallic silver is formed. Formaldehyde has a destructive influence on the lower forms of life, i. e. bacteria and molds, and is much used as a disinfectant.

Ketones. The ketones are formed by the oxidation of secondary alcohols. They have the general formula R_2CO.

Acetone $CH_3 . CO . CH_3$ is the best known of the ketones. It is obtained from crude wood spirits, one of the products of the destructive distillation of wood. Technically it is prepared by the distillation of calcium acetate.

Acetone shows the general properties of the ketones. It is used as a solvent and in the manufacture of sulphonal, chloroform and iodoform.

A knowledge of the general properties of aldehydes and ketones is very important in food chemistry since the simple sugars are either aldehyde or ketone derivatives and therefore show many of the properties of these bodies. In the tables below a list of the more important properties of the aldehydes and ketones is given.

Reagent	Aldehydes	Ketones
Reducing agents (sodium amalgam and water, Zn and HCl)	form primary alcohols	form secondary alcohols
Oxidizing agents	form acids of same number of carbon atoms.	form acids each containing less **no.** of carbon atoms
Fehling's solution	reduced by aldehydes	not reduced by ketones
Amm. silver nitrate	reduced by aldehydes	not reduced by ketones
Phenylhydrazine	form hydrazones	form hydrazones

Experiment No. 9.—Formaldehyde

Reading—P. & K. pp. 118-122.
            N. pp. 170 176.

Apparatus.—4 test-tubes, beaker, 2 watch glasses, platinum wire.

Material.—Formalin, ammonical silver nitrate, Fehling's solution, milk, cotton wool, lime water, phenolphthalein solution, methyl alcohol.

Preparation. Prepare some formaldehyde as follows: Place 10 cc. of methyl alcohol in a small beaker; heat a spiral of platinum wire to dull redness in a flame and quickly suspend the heated wire over the alcohol. Notice the odor of the vapors which are evolved. Generally a slight explosion occurs.

Tests. Use Formalin, for these tests.

1.—Add a few drops of formalin to 5 cc. of water in a test-tube; pour in a few drops of an ammoniacal solution of silver nitrate and warm gently. The formation of a silver mirror on the bottom of the test-tube shows the reducing property of the aldehyde.

2.—Add a drop of formalin to 5 cc. of Fehling's solution * in a test-tube, and heat to boiling. The brick red precipitate, (cuprous oxide), is formed as a result of the action of the aldehyde on the copper hydroxide. Fehling's solution is an alkaline tartrate solution of copper hydroxide. The aldehyde reduces the copper hydroxide to cuprous oxide.

3.—Fill two test-tubes two-thirds full of fresh milk and label the tubes A and B. To A add a few drops of formalin and mix well. Plug both tubes with cotton wool and allow to stand for 24 hours at room temperature; then examine each tube and note odor, coagulation and acidity. Make the acidity test as follows: **A**dd enough lime water to 10 cc. of phenolphthalein solution to produce a faint pink color; pour 5 cc. into each of two watch glasses. To one watch glass add the milk from **A**, and to

---

* Note. Fehling's solution is an alkaline tartrate solution of copper hydroxide. It is made up in two parts, A, and B: B is a solution of potassium or sodium hydroxide and Rochelle salts (sodium potassium tartrate) and A is a solution of copper sulphate. For use equal parts of A and B are mixed.

the other add the milk from B. Add the milk carefully, a few drops at a time, and see if, in either case, the phenolphthalein solution is decolorized. Unless too much lime water has been added to the phenolphthalein solution, this test will serve to show the presence of a slight amount of acid in the milk. Can you tell which test-tube contains the most acid? Why is formaldehyde considered a good disinfectant?

Experiment No. 10—Acetone

Reading—P. & K. pp. 130-145.
        N. p. 187.

Apparatus. Hard glass test-tube, clamp, distilling apparatus, 2 test-tubes, Bunsen burner.

Material. Barium acetate, ammoniacal silver nitrate, Fehling's solution.

Prepration. Place 15g. of powdered barium acetate in a large hard glass test-tube and connect with a condenser. Clamp the test-tube in a horizontal position. Heat the test-tube containing the acetate strongly but evenly. When two or three cc. of distillate have been obtained stop the distillation. The distillate contains acetone mixed with water and other impurities. Use distillate for the tests.

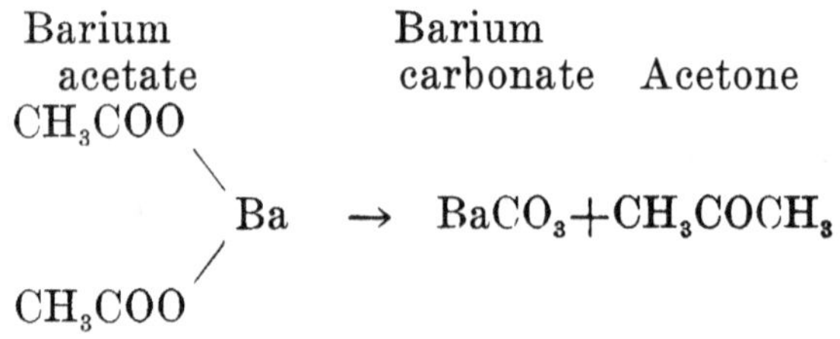

Tests.

1.—What are the physical properties of acetone?
2.—Use a few drops of the distillate and make tests 1 and 2 given under aldehyde.

CHAPTER VI

Acids

Fatty Acids. The acids derived from the paraffins are called fatty acids because many of the acids which enter into the composition of the fats belong to this series. Fatty acids are formed by the complete oxidation of primary alcohols. The relation between the paraffin, alcohol and acid is shown in the table given in chapter II. The most important fatty acids are given below.

Formic—$HCOOH$
Acetic—CH_3COOH
Propionic—C_2H_5COOH
Butyric—C_3H_7COOH
Caproic—$C_5H_{11}COOH$
Caprylic—$C_7H_{15}COOH$
Capric—$C_9H_{19}COOH$
Lauric—$C_{11}H_{23}COOH$
Myristic—$C_{13}H_{27}COOH$
Palmitic—$C_{15}H_{31}COOH$
Stearic—$C_{17}H_{35}COOH$

The first member of the series, formic acid, is formed by the oxidation of methyl alcohol. Acetic acid, the acid in vinegar, is formed from ethyl alcohol. Propionic acid is likewise prepared from its corresponding alcohol. Butyric acid is practically prepared by the butyric acid fermentation of glucose. It can be obtained in small amounts from butter fats. Palmitic and stearic acids are obtained by the hydrolysis of the fats, especially suet and tallow. Oleic acid, $C_{17}H_{33}COOH$, an unsaturated acid, is obtained from these fats and also from lard, olive oil, cotton seed oil and other oils.

Experiment No. 11.—Acetic acid

Reading—P. & K. pp. 145-156.
          N. p. 220-227.

Apparatus. Round bottom flask (250cc.), reflux condenser, sand bath, ringstand, wire gauze, Bunsen burner, beaker, 2 test tubes.

Material. Potassium bichromate, conc. sulphuric acid,
alcohol, sodium hydroxide, ferric chloride.

Preparation. Garrett and Harden-Practical Organic
Chemistry, p. 39. ''Place 30g. of coarsely powdered
potassium bichromate in a round-bottomed flask,
and add a cold mixture of 30g. conc. sulphuric acid
with 18cc. of water; place the flask on a sand
bath and connect it with a back flow condenser, and
then add gradually 5cc. of alcohol diluted with an
equal volume of water. After each addition, a vigorous reaction takes place, and the liquid becomes
very hot; allow all action to cease before adding the
next quantity, but do not cool the flask. When all
the alcohol has been added, boil for ten minutes, then
connect the flask with the other end of the condenser
and distill over wire gauze, until about 20cc. of distillate have come over. This consists of aqueous
acetic acid, but usually also smells slightly of acetic
ether and aldehyde.'' Use distillate for the tests.

$$3C_2H_5OH + 2K_2Cr_2O_7 + 10H_2SO_4 \rightarrow 4KHSO_4$$

$$+ 2Cr_2(SO_4)_3 + 3\,C_2H_4O_2 + 11\,H_2O$$

where $3C_2H_5OH$ is Alcohol, $2K_2Cr_2O_7$ is Potassium bichromate, $10H_2SO_4$ is Sulphuric acid, $4KHSO_4$ is Potassium bisulphate, $2Cr_2(SO_4)_3$ is Chromium sulphate, $3\,C_2H_4O_2$ is Acetic acid, and $11\,H_2O$ is Water.

Tests.

1.—Describe the odor of acetic acid.

2.—Carefully neutralize a portion of the distillate
with sodium hydroxide, and then add a few drops of fer-

ric chloride. The red coloration indicates the presence of the acetate. Repeat this test with a few drops of uncolored vinegar instead of the distillate.

3.—Take 4cc. of the distillate and add 1cc. of alcohol and 2cc. of conc. sulphuric acid. Mix well and then determine the odor. Acetic ether is formed and may be recognized by its odor.

Questions.

1.—How is vinegar prepared commercially? In this case what is the oxidizing agent?

CHAPTER VII

Esters

Esters. Esters are acid derivatives formed by replacing the hydrogen of the carboxyl group of the acid by some hydrocarbon radical. If the acid is an organic acid the ester will have the general formula $RCOOR$. The esters are named according to the acids from which they are derived. The ethyl ester of nitric acid is ethyl nitrate, $C_2H_5NO_3$, of acetic acid, ethyl acetate, $CH_3COOC_2H_5$. The esters are prepared by several different methods. A general method for their formation is by the condensation between an acid and an alcohol. Sulphuric acid is generally used as the condensation agent.

$$\text{Fatty acid} \quad \text{Alcohol} \quad \text{Ester} \quad \text{Water}$$
$$RCOOH + ROH \xrightarrow{H_2SO_4} RCOOR + H_2O$$

When esters are heated with water, dilute acids, and alkalies, they are hydrolized with the formation of the free acid, or salt of the acid, and the alcohol. **This reaction** is spoken of as **saponification** because it is the reaction used in soap making.

$$\text{Ester} \quad \text{Acid} \quad \text{Alcohol}$$
$$RCOOR + H_2O \rightarrow RCOOH + ROH$$

The esters are used in the manufacture of artificial fruit flavorings. Ethyl butyrate, $C_3H_7COOC_2H_5$, is used for pineapple flavor. Pentyl acetate, $CH_3COOC_5H_{11}$, is used as pear flavor. Banana essence is made up of pentyl acetate and ethyl butyrate, and apple essence is composed of pentyl valerianate, $C_4H_9COOC_5H_{11}$.

Experiment No. 12—Esters

Reading—P. & K. pp. 174, 188-193.
   N. pp. 278-280.

Apparatus. 2 test-tubes, Bunsen burner.

Material. Alcohol, acetic acid, conc. sulphuric acid, butyric acid.

Ethyl Acetate. In a test-tube mix 5cc. of alcohol with an equal amount of acetic acid; add a few drops of conc. sulphuric acid and warm gently. Notice the odor.

$$CH_3COOH + C_2H_5OH \rightarrow CH_3COOC_2H_5 + H_2O.$$

Ethyl Butyrate. Place one drop of butyric acid in 5cc. of water, add a few drops of conc. sulphuric acid and then 1cc. of alcohol. Mix and warm gently. Ethyl butyrate has the odor of pineapple. Do you distinguish this odor in the test-tube?

$$C_3H_7COOH + C_2H_5OH \rightarrow C_3H_7COOC_2H_5 + H_2O.$$

CHAPTER VIII.

Fats

Fats. The fats are glyceryl esters of the fatty acids. They may be represented by the general formula $(RCOO)_3C_3H_5$.

When saponified the fats yield the free fatty acid, or its salt, and glycerine. Glycerine it will be remembered is a trihydric alcohol.

$$\text{Fat} \qquad\qquad \text{Fatty acid} \qquad \text{Glycerine}$$
$$(RCOO)_3C_3H_5 + 3H_2O \rightarrow 3RCOOH \ + \ C_3H_5(OH)_3$$

The most important fats are stearin, $(C_{17}H_{35}COO)_3C_3H_5$, palmitin, $(C_{15}H_{31}COO)_3C_3H_5$, and olein, $(C_{17}H_{33}COO)_3C_3H_5$. These occur in the animal fats such as suet, tallow, lard, and butter, and in many of the vegetable fats such as sesmane oil, cottonseed oil, peanut oil, etc. Stearin does not occur in olive oil but the other fats do.

Experiment No. 13.—Fats

Reading—P. & K. pp. 169-174.
Leach, pp. 471-480.
Sherman, pp. 16-17, pp. 20-23.

Apparatus. Basin, capillary tubes, thermometer, beakers, test-tubes, Bunsen burner.

Material. Tallow, lard, suet, butter, olive oil, muslin bag, soap solution, alcohol, chloroform, ether, benzene, litmus paper, potassium bisulphate.

Tests.

1.—**Melting Point.** Place a muslin bag containing about 2g. of tallow in a pan of hot water and squeeze out the melted fat; allow the water to cool, then skim off the solid fat from the surface. Dry the fat between filter paper. Refine a small amount of suet in the same way. Determine the melting point of the suet and tallow and, also, of some butter and lard as follows:

Place a beaker partly filled with water in a second beaker of water, the two vessels being separated by pieces of cork. Fill a capillary tube with the fat which is to be tested; attach the capillary tube to a thermometer inserted in a cork; suspend thermometer in the inner beaker of water. Now gently heat the beakers of water over a wire gauze and note the temperature at which the fat melts.

Fill out the following record:

Fat	Melting Point
Lard	
Tallow	
Butter	
Suet	

2.—**Solubility.** Test the solubility of olive oil in hot and cold water, in soap solution, and in alcohol, chloroform, ether and benzene. **(Avoid flame when using alcohol, ether and benzene.)**

3.—**Rancidity.** Test the reaction of some old olive oil and old butter to litmus paper.

4.—**Acrolein Test.** Grind up a small piece of tallow in a mortar with an equal bulk of dry potassium bisulphate; transfer to a test-tube and heat until dense white fumes are evolved. Observe the odor of the fumes taking care however not to get them in the eyes. The irritating odor of the fumes is due to acrolein, a product resulting from the decomposition of glycerine. Do you get this same odor when fats are heated too strongly?

Questions.

1. What causes fats to become rancid?
2.—What is ''process'' butter?

3.—What is oleomargine? Is it a good substitute **for** butter?

4.—Of what are the "compound" lards composed?

5.—What chemical compound is formed when fats are too highly heated as sometimes happens in deep **fat** cookery?

6.—How would you remove a grease stain from non-washable fabrics?

CHAPTER IX.

Soap and Glycerine

Soaps. When fat is boiled with a solution of sodium or potassium hydroxide the fat is hydrolized with the formation of soap and glycerine. If the alkali used is potassium hydroxide, soft soap is formed. If sodium hydroxide is used a hard soap will result. Both the animal fats and vegetable oils are used in soap making. The vegetable oils produce a less caustic soap.

Glycerine. Glycerine is formed when fats are saponified. After the soap is removed the watery solution is evaporated and the glycerine is purified by distillation under diminished pressure. Glycerine is a sweet colorless syrup which mixes with water and alcohol in every proportion. When glycerine is heated with a dehydrating substance, such as potassium bisulphate, it undergoes decomposition into water and acrolein. **A**crolein is an aldehyde.

Acrolein reaction

Glycerine   Acrolein

$$C_3H_5(OH)_3 \rightarrow CH_2.CH.CHO + 2H_2O$$

Experiment No. 14.—Soap and Glycerine

Reading—P. & K. pp. 171-172.

Apparatus. 500cc. flask, evaporating dish, stirring rod, burner, ring-stand, beaker, 4 test-tubes.

Material. Lard, alcohol, potassium hydroxide, 90 per cent alcohol, absolute alcohol, dilute sulphuric acid, sodium carbonate, potassium bi-sulphate, calcium sulphate solution, magnesium sulphate solution, dilute hydrochloric acid.

Saponification of **Lard.** Dissolve 25g. of lard in an equal volume of alcohol by warming in a flask on a water bath, add 75cc. of alcoholic potassium hydroxide, (**10g.** of potassium hydroxide dissolved in 10cc. of water and diluted to 75cc. with 90 per cent alcohol), and heat on the water-bath until all the fat is saponified. This can be ascertained by pouring a drop or two of the mixture into a test-tube of water. When saponification is complete the mixture will dissolve with no separation of free fat. Now transfer the solution from the flask to an evaporating dish containing 100cc. of water and heat on the water-bath until all the alcohol is driven off. Acidify the solution with dilute hydrochloric acid, and cool. The fatty acids separate out and rise to the surface. Skim off the precipitated fatty acids and save for the preparation of soap. Save the solution in the evaporating dish for the extraction of glycerine.

$$(C_{15}H_{31}COO)_3C_3H_5 + 3H_2O \rightarrow 3C_{15}H_{31}COOH + C_3H_5(OH)_3$$

Preparation of **Soap.** Melt the precipitated fatty acids in a beaker on the water-bath; add, gradually with constant stirring, a half saturated solution of sodium carbonate until the fatty acids have dissolved. This will take some time. Avoid an excess of sodium carbonate. As soon as solution has taken place, allow to stand until cold. The solid residue is soap. Press into a cake and save for tests.

$$2C_{15}H_{31}COOH + Na_2CO_3 \rightarrow 2C_{15}H_{31}COONa + H_2O + CO_2$$

Tests for **Soap.** Dissolve a portion of the soap in water and use this solution for the tests.

1.—Place 5cc. of the soap solution in a test-tube and add a few drops of dilute sulphuric acid. The curdy precipitate is free fatty acid.

2.—To 5cc. of the soap solution in a test-tube, add a few drops of calcium sulphate solution. The precipitate is a calcium soap.

3.—Repeat test 2, using magnesium suphate solution

instead of calcium sulphate. What is the effect of hard water on soap solutions?

Extraction of **Glycerine.** Use the solution saved from the saponification test. Neutralize the solution with sodium carbonate and evaporate to dryness on the water-bath. Extract the residue with absolute alcohol, remove the alcohol by evaporation on the water-bath, and, with the residue of glycerine thus obtained, make the tests given below.

Tests for **Glycerine.**

1.—Describe the taste of the glycerine.

2.—Place some of the glycerine in a dry test-tube and add a pinch of dry potassium bisulphate. Heat cautiously and notice the fumes of acrolein which are evolved. Avoid getting the fumes into the eyes.

Questions.

1.—How is soap made in the home?

2.—How are toilet soaps made?

3.—To what is the cleansing action of soap due?

4.—Why should hard water be softened before being used for laundry purposes? How may water be softened?

CHAPTER X.

Simple Sugars

Carbohydrates. The sugars are the simplest of the carbohydrates. All the carbohydrates are called saccharides. The simple sugars are called monosaccharides. The more complex sugars are grouped as di- and tri-saccharides according as they yield two or three molecules of monosaccharides on decomposition. Carbohydrates which decompose into several molecules of monosaccharide compounds are named polysaccharides.

Classification of Carbohydrates.

Sugars.

    I.   Monosaccharides: pentoses, hexoses (glucose, fructose, etc.)

    II.   Disaccharides: cane sugar, malt sugar, milk sugar, etc.

    III.   Trisaccharides: raffinose.

    IV.   Polysaccharides.

        1.   Starches.

        2.   Gums.

        3.   Celluloses.

Monosaccharides. The monosaccharides or simple sugars, are aldehyde or ketone derivatives of polyhydric alcohols. They are named from the number of carbon atoms which they contain and are given the terminal ending ose. Thus, sugars whose molecules are built up of six carbon atoms are called hexoses, those containing five are pentoses, etc. The most important group of the monosaccharides is the hexose, $C_6H_{12}O_6$, group to which glucose and fructose belong.

Glucose. Glucose, or grape sugar, formerly called dextrose, occurs in many sweet fruits and in honey. It is found in the urine in cases of **Diabetes mellitus.** It is formed when the polysaccharides, (cane sugar, starch, cellulose), are hydrolized. It is also formed by the decomposition of the glucosides. Glucose is prepared commercially by boiling starch with dilute sulphuric acid.

Glucose crystallizes from water in nodular masses, melting at 86°. It is soluble in its own weight of water. Glucose is not as sweet as cane sugar.

Glucose is an aldehyde sugar.

Glucose resembles both aldehydes and polyhydric alcohols in its chemical behavior. It shows the following characteristic aldehyde reactions:

1.—On reduction glucose is converted into a hexahydric alcohol.

2.—On oxidation glucose is converted into an acid containing six carbon atoms, gluconic acid.

3.—Glucose precipitates cuprous oxide from alkaline cupric solutions. 0.05 grams of glucose exactly reduce 10cc. of Fehling's solution.

4.—Glucose reduces an ammoniacal solution of silver nitrate.

5.—With excess of phenylhydrazine glucose forms glucosazone.

Glucose resembles the alcohols in that it reacts with organic acids to form esters, the most important of which are the **glucosides** obtained from plants. Salicin, amygdalin, coniferin, and tannins are examples of glucosides. The tannins are grape-sugar esters of the tannic acids.

Glucose ferments readily with yeast yielding alcohol and carbon dioxide as the main products. Under the influence of certain bacteria glucose undergoes a lactic acid fermentation. This is the fermentation which occurs in the souring of bread, the souring of milk and in the manufacture of dill pickles and sauerkraut.

Alcoholic fermentation

glucose zymase   alcohol carbon dioxide

$$C_6H_{12}O_6 \longrightarrow 2\ C_2H_5OH + 2CO_2$$

Lactic acid fermentation

lactic acid

glucose   ferment   lactic acid

$$C_6H_{12}O_6 \longrightarrow 2\ C_3H_6O_3$$

Glucose is most frequently placed on the market in the form of a syrup. It is used extensively in the manufacture of jellies, jams, confectionery and canned products.

Fructose. Fructose, fruit sugar, levulose, $C_6H_{12}O_6$, occurs together with glucose in almost all sweet fruits. It may be obtained by the hydrolytic decomposition of inulin, a starch found in the roots of the dahlia and some other plants. It is formed in equal amounts with glucose when cane sugar is hydrolized. Fructose is a ketone sugar.

Fructose is more soluble in water than glucose and crystallizes less readily. It separates out from alcohol in small hard crystals which melt at 95°.

Fructose resembles glucose in chemical behavior. It reduces Fehling's solution to the same extent as glucose. With excess of phenylhydrazine it forms glucosazone. It differs from glucose in the solubility of its lime compound. On oxidation fructose gives the characteristic ketone reaction, i. e. forms acids of less carbon content. Fructose when oxidized with nitric acid gives glycollic acid, CH_2OH, and tartaric acid, $CHOHCOOH$.

$$\underset{\displaystyle COOH}{\overset{\displaystyle CH_2OH}{\big|}} \qquad\qquad \underset{\displaystyle CHOHCOOH}{\overset{\displaystyle CHOHCOOH}{\big|}}$$

Experiment No. 15—Glucose and Fructose

Reading—P. & K. pp. 266-274.
      N. pp. 357-366.
      Sherman pp. 4-9.

Apparatus. 4 beakers, water-bath. carbon di-oxide generator, 6 test-tubes, 2 evaporating dishes, burner.

Material. Sugar, dilute sulphuric acid, chalk, slaked lime, ice, filter paper, conc. hydrochloric acid, marble, Fehling's solution, potassium hydroxide, lime water, glucose, phenylhydrazine hydrochloride, sodium acetate, conc. sulphuric acid, honey, raisins, apples.

Preparation of Glucose and Fructose. Dissolve 10g. of sugar in 50cc. of water in a beaker and add 15cc. of dilute sulphuric acid; heat on a water-bath at 70° for 20 minutes; cool, exactly neutralize with chalk; filter off the precipitated calcium sulphate. Place filtrate in a beaker, cool with ice, and add 6g. of slaked lime, in small quantities at a time, stirring constantly. Keep the beaker cold and allow to stand for a few minutes. The lime compound of fructose is insoluble and will separate out as a pasty precipitate. Filter and use precipitate for fructose extraction and filtrate for the extraction of glucose. Label the filtrate A, and save until you are ready to extract glucose.

Suspend the lime-fructose precipitate in 50cc. of water in a beaker and run in carbon di-oxide gas until the mixture is no longer alkaline. Filter off the precipitated calcium carbonate, and evaporate the filtrate to a thick syrup on a water-bath. The syrup consists of nearly pure fructose. Use this syrup for the fructose tests.

Extract the glucose from filtrate A by passing in carbon di-oxide gas until the solution no longer reacts alkaline; then filter and evaporate to a thick syrup on the water-bath. Use syrup for glucose tests.

$$\underset{\text{cane sugar}}{C_{12}H_{22}O_{11}} \;+\; \underset{\text{water}}{H_2O} \;\rightarrow\; \underset{\text{glucose}}{C_6H_{12}O_6} \;+\; \underset{\text{fructose}}{C_6H_{12}O_6}$$

Tests for Glucose.

1.—Taste the glucose syrup and compare sweetness with that of cane sugar. Dissolve the syrup in about 10cc. of water and use the solution for tests 2, 3 and 4.

2.—To about 2cc. of the glucose solution add a few drops of conc. sulphuric acid. Does any change occur? Warm and notice that the solution becomes yellow at first and finally darkens.

3.—Add a few drops of the glucose solution to 5cc. of Fehling's solution in a test-tube. Boil and describe the changes which take place. Is the color due to the precipitate, or to the solution?

4.—Add a few drops of clear lime water to about 5cc. of the glucose solution. Mix well. Is there a precipitate formed?

5.—Dissolve 1g. of solid glucose, (grape-sugar), and 3g. of sodium acetate in 20cc. of water in a beaker; add 2g. of phenylhydrazine hydrochloride and mix well. Heat the mixture on the water-bath at boiling temperature for 20 minutes. On cooling a yellow crystalline precipitate, glucosazone, is obtained.

Tests for Fructose.

Repeat tests 1, 2, 3 and 4, given under glucose, using the fructose syrup and solution instead of glucose. In what way does fructose differ from glucose?

Tests for Glucose and Fructose in Foods.

Make a water extract of raisins, of honey, and of apples. In each case test the solution with Fehling's solution. Do these substances contain reducing sugars?

Questions.

1.—Of what importance is glucose commercially? How is commercial glucose prepared?

2.—What is corn syrup?

3.—Are candies and preserves made of glucose wholesome?

4.—Would glucose or fructose be a good substitute for cane sugar?

Experiment No. 16.—Determination of the Amount of Reducing Sugar in a Sample of Syrup or Molasses

Reading.—Leach. pp. 590-593.

Apparatus. 2 100 cc. graduated flasks, 2 burettes, Erlenmeyer flask (250 cc.), ring-stand, wire gauze, burner.

Material.—Syrup or molasses, lead subacetate solution, sodium sulphate solution, standard Fehling's solution, anhydrous dextrose.

Standardization of Fehling's Solution.

Make up Fehling's solution in two parts as follows:

A. Fehling's Copper Solution.—34.639 g. of crystals of pure copper sulphate, powdered, dissolved in water and diluted to exactly 500 cc. .

B. Fehling's Alkaline Tartrate Solution—173 g. of Rochelle salts and 50 g. of sodium hydroxide dissolved in water and diluted to exactly 500 cc. .

Dissolve 0.5 g. of pure anhydrous dextrose in a little water in a 100 cc. graduated flask and dilute to exactly 100 cc. Mix thoroughly and fill a clean, dry burette with this solution. With pipettes add 5 cc. of Fehling's solution A, and 5 cc. of solution B to a 250 cc. Erlenmeyer flask; add 40 cc. of water and boil over a wire gauze. While still boiling, add from burette a measured quantity of the dextrose solution. Boil three minutes after each addition of dextrose. Run in the dextrose solution until the copper is all reduced to cuprous oxide. The end-point must be very carefully determined. As the sugar is added and the solution boiled, several changes of color occur; the solution is first deep blue, then appears to be green, dull red and finally brick red. The green and red color is produced by the precipitate. The solution is blue as long as there is any unreduced copper; when all the copper has been reduced to cuprous oxide, the solution becomes colorless or yellow. The difficulty in determining the end point exactly is due to the fact that the red precipitate obscures the real color of the solution. Leach, (Food Analysis, pp. 591, 592,), recommends that, as soon as the dull red tint is obtained, the sugar be added a little at a time; after each addition has been added and boiled he recommends that the flask be removed from the flame and the bright diffused light from a window be viewed through the solution with the eye on a level with the surface. If this is done a thin line will be observed just below the surface of the solution. This line will be blue as long as there is unreduced copper in the solution. When, however, all the copper has been reduced, this line ceases to be blue and becomes yellow or colorless.

When the end point has been reached, calculate the strength of your Fehling's solution in grams of glucose. If 0.5g. of dextrose are diluted to 100cc., 1cc. of the solution will contain how many grams of dextrose?

10cc. of your Fehling's solution are equivalent to how many grams of dextrose?

$$10cc. \text{ Fehling's solution} = \text{ ? g. dextrose}$$

Determination of the amount of reducing sugar (calculated as dextrose), in a sample of syrup or molasses.

Weigh 5g. of molasses or syrup into a 100cc. graduated flask. Dissolve in a little water. In the case of molasses or "golden" syrup it is necessary to decolorize by the addition of lead subacetate solution. Add from 2 to 5cc. of the subacetate solution to precipitate the coloring matter. Make up to the 100cc. mark with water, filter; take 25cc. of the filtrate and, if lead subacetate has been added, precipitate the excess of lead with sodium sulphate solution; filter; then dilute to 100cc. with water. This diluted solution should not contain more than $\frac{1}{2}$ per cent of dextrose. Fill a clean, dry burette with this solution and determine how much it takes to reduce exactly 10cc. of Fehling's solution. Make the determination in the same way as in the standardization of the Fehling's solution. Determine the end-point carefully. From the data at hand calculate the amount of reducing sugar, (dextrose), in the syrup.

Substitute your own figures and tabulate the result as follows:

10 cc. of Fehling's solution = ...no. cc. of syrup solution

10 cc. of Fehling's solution = 0.05 grams of dextrose

....no. cc. of syrup solution=0.05 grams of dextrose

1 cc. of syrup solution=....grams of dextrose

Syrup solution=? per cent dextrose

CHAPTER XI

Disaccharides

Cane Sugar. Cane sugar, sucrose, $C_{12}H_{22}O_{11}$, is by far the most important of all the sugars. The annual consumption amounts to about 80 pounds per capita. It is obtained from the sugar cane, sugar beet, sorghum cane, and from maple sap. It occurs in the juice of sweet fruits, such as the pine-apple, in vegetables, such as the carrot, and in all cereals.

Cane sugar is very soluble in water and crystallizes out in well defined prisms. When melted and allowed to cool it forms a clear yellow mass called barley sugar. Barley sugar slowly changes back to the crystalline form.

At high temperatures cane sugar is decomposed yielding water and carbon. The first stage in its decomposition results in the formation of caramel.

Disaccharide sugars are so named because, when boiled with acids, or acted upon by ferments, they yield two parts of a monosaccharide sugar. Cane sugar forms glucose and fructose.

$$\overset{\text{cane sugar}}{C_{12}H_{22}O_{11}} + H_2O \;\rightarrow\; \overset{\text{glucose}}{C_6H_{12}O_6} \;+\; \overset{\text{fructose}}{C_6H_{12}O_6}$$

This reaction is spoken of as the inversion of cane sugar and the resulting mixture of glucose and fructose is called invert sugar. In cookery the inversion occurs whenever cane sugar is cooked with acid substances such as vinegar, fruit juices, or cream of tartar. Invert sugar does not crystallize as readily as cane sugar.

Cane sugar does not ferment directly but must first be inverted. Ordinary yeast secretes a ferment, invertase, which causes the inversion. The invert sugar then undergoes alcoholic fermentation through the influence of another ferment, zymase.

$$\text{C}_{12}\text{H}_{22}\text{O}_{11}+\text{H}_2\text{O} \xrightarrow{\text{invertase}} \text{C}_6\text{H}_{12}\text{O}_6+\text{C}_6\text{H}_{12}\text{O}_6$$

$$2\text{C}_6\text{H}_{12}\text{O}_6 \xrightarrow{\text{zymase}} 4\text{C}_2\text{H}_5\text{O H}+4\text{CO}_2$$

Experiment No. 17.—Cane Sugar

Reading—P. & K. pp. 274-276.
   N. pp. 367-370.
   Sherman, pp. 9-11.

Apparatus. Porcelain or enamel casserole ($\frac{1}{2}$ pint), 4 test-tubes, beaker, burner, ring-stand, wire gauze, candy thermometer.

Material. Sugar, Fehling's solution, dilute hydrochloric acid, sodium hydroxide, concentrated sulphuric acid, yeast.

Tests: Prepare an aqueous solution of sugar and use for the first four tests.

1.—To 5cc. of sugar solution add an equal volume of concentrated sulphuric acid. What is the result? How does glucose differ from cane sugar in respect to this test?

2.—Add a few drops of the sugar solution to 10cc. of Fehling's solution and heat. Is cane sugar a reducing sugar?

3.—To 5cc. of sugar solution add 1cc. of dilute hydrochloric acid and boil for a few minutes. Cool, neutralize with a few drops of dilute sodium hydroxide and test with Fehling's solution. What change has taken place in the sugar?

4.—Add a little yeast to about 5cc. of the sugar solution in a test-tube; mix well and allow to stand for 15 minutes; filter and test with Fehling's solution. Invertase, an enzyme secreted by yeast, acts upon cane sugar converting it into glucose and fructose.

5.—Carefully heat some sugar in a casserole until

the sugar just melts. Stir to prevent burning. With a candy thermometer, (or ordinary high temperature thermometer), ascertain the temperature of the melted sugar. Pour some of the melted sugar on a glass plate; when cool, examine and taste.

6.—Heat the remainder of the sugar in the casserole to about 200°. As soon as the substance appears to boil, remove from flame, cool, examine and taste. What is formed?

Questions.

1.—How is caramel prepared? For what is it used?

2.—What is peanut "brittle"?

3.—In making jelly is it better to add the sugar in the beginning, or after boiling the juice?

4.—Why is cane sugar added to the dough in making bread? Could glucose be added instead?

5.—Why is cream of tartar added in making fondant?

6.—Is cane sugar superior to the same grade of beet sugar? Describe the commercial preparation of each.

7.—What is powdered sugar? Is it less sweet than granulated sugar?

Malt Sugar. Malt sugar, maltose, $C_{12}H_{22}O_{11}$, is formed by the action of malt diastase on starch. Malt diatase is a ferment which occurs in germinating grains, especially barley.

$$\underset{\text{starch}}{3(C_6H_{10}O_5)n} + nH_2O \xrightarrow{\text{malt diastase}} \underset{\text{maltose}}{nC_{12}H_{22}O_{11}} + \underset{\text{dextrin}}{nC_{36}H_{60}O_{30}}$$

The same reaction occurs during digestion under the influence of ptyalin and amylopsin.

Maltose ferments readily with yeast yielding alcohol and carbon dioxide as the chief products.

$$\underset{\text{maltose}}{C_{12}H_{22}O_{11}} + \underset{\text{water}}{H_2O} \rightarrow \underset{\text{alcohol}}{4\,C_2H_5OH} + \underset{\text{carbon dioxide}}{4\,CO_2}$$

Experiment No. 18—Malt sugar

Reading.—P. & K. pp. 276-277.

N. p. 370.

Sherman, p. 11.

Apparatus. Pan, water-bath, evaporating dish, test-tube.

Material. Barley, filter paper, Fehling's solution.

Preparation. Line a pan or pneumatic trough with moist filter paper; cover the bottom of the pan with barley, moisten well, and keep in a warm place for two or three days. Do not allow the barley to become dry. When the barley is well sprouted, remove from pan, and dry in the oven or on a sand bath. Be careful not to heat the sprouts over 100°. Cover the dry sprouts with water and macerate in a mortar; strain through muslin, then filter. Use filtrate for tests.

Tests.

1.—Place 5cc. of the filtrate in a test-tube and make Fehling's test.

2.—Evaporate the remainder of the filtrate to a thick syrup over the water-bath. Study the properties of the syrup.

Questions.

1.—Of what commercial value is malt sugar?

2.—How is malt sugar manufactured?

Milk Sugar. Milk sugar, lactose, $C_{12}H_{22}O_{11}$, is sometimes called animal sugar because, so far as is known, it occurs only in the animal kingdom. It is obtained from milk as a by-product in the manufacture of cheese.

Milk sugar differs materially from cane sugar both in physical and chemical properties. When boiled with acids it yields glucose and galactose.

$$\underset{\text{lactose}}{C_{12}H_{22}O_{11}}+H_2O\rightarrow\underset{\text{glucose}}{C_6H_{12}O_6}+\underset{\text{galactose}}{C_6H_{12}O_6}$$

Milk sugar does not ferment with yeast. Under the influence of a ferment secreted by certain bacteria, which are normally present in milk, it undergoes lactic acid fermentation.

$$\underset{\text{lactose}}{C_{12}H_{22}O_{11}} + H_2O \rightarrow \underset{\text{lactic acid}}{4C_3H_6O_3}$$

Experiment No. 19.—Milk sugar

Reading.—P. & K. p. 277.
   N. p. 370.
   Sherman, p. 11.

Apparatus. Beaker, water-bath, ring-stand, burner, test-tube, evaporating dish, glass rod.

Material. Milk, rennet extract, Fehling's solution.

Extraction From Milk. Place a beaker containing 500cc. of milk in a water-bath and warm to about 40°; add 10 drops of rennet extract to the milk and let stand in the warm water until a solid clot forms. Break the clot up with a glass rod and separate curd from whey by straining through a muslin cloth. Put whey in a beaker and boil over a wire gauze until the albumin is precipitated; filter, and evaporate the filtrate to a thin syrup on the water-bath. Allow the syrup to stand until crystallization occurs. Use the crystallized product for the tests.

Tests.

1.—Taste some of the milk sugar and compare sweetness with cane sugar.

2.—Dissolve some of the sugar in water and make Fehling's test.

Questions.

1.—How is the milk sugar of commerce obtained?
2.—Can milk sugar be obtained from sour milk?
3.—Why is milk sugar added in modifying cow's milk for infants? Could cane sugar be used instead?

CHAPTER XII

Starches

Starch. Ordinary starch, amylum, $(C_6H_{10}O_5)_n$, occurs in all green plants. It is stored in the seeds, roots and tubers of plants. We obtain it from cereals, from corn, and from potatoes and arrow root. It is in the form of minute granules consisting of starch cells inclosed in a cell wall. The physical structure of the granules is different in different plants. By means of the microscope we may determine the source of the starch, that is, whether it is from corn, potato, or some other plant. The microscope is of value in detecting the use of starch as an adulterant in foods.

Starch is insoluble in cold water. When boiling water is poured over starch the granules are broken and the contents dissolve. The cellulose walls of the granules remain in suspension in the solution and form a gelatinous mixture called starch paste.

Dry heat converts starch into dextrin. The dextrins are gums. They dissolve in water forming a mucilaginous solution. Several dextrins are known, **amylodextrin** which gives a purple color with iodine solution, **erythrodextrin** which reacts with iodine to form a **mahogany-red** coloration, and **achroodextrin** which is colorless with iodine. Dextrins are intermediate products formed in the conversion of starch into sugar. Some dextrinization always occurs when starch foods are baked.

When starch solution is boiled with an acid the starch is converted into dextrin, maltose, and finally glucose. Commercial glucose which is prepared in this way is generally a mixture of these three compounds.

Starch gives a characteristic reaction with a solution of iodine in potassium iodide. This reaction is made use of in the identification of starch.

Experiment No. 20.—Starch

Reading.—P. & K. pp. 278-280.
      N. p. 373.
      Sherman, pp. 12-14.

Apparatus. Pan, beaker (8oz.), beaker (6oz.), evaporating dish, 4 test-tubes, glass slides, microscope, mortar.

Material. Potatoes, iodine solution (2g. of iodine and 4g. of potassium iodide in 100cc. of water), Fehling's solution, dilute hydrochloric acid, conc. nitric acid, bread, corn, sago, rice, bean, arrow-root starch.

Extraction.—Grate 4 medium sized potatoes and place the pulp in a muslin bag in a pan of water; squeeze out the milky juice. Allow to stand until the starch has settled to the bottom of the pan, then pour off the water, and wash the starch by decantation. Dry the starch between filter paper and use for tests.

Tests.

1.—Prepare a starch solution as follows: Make a paste of 1g. of starch and 2cc. of water in a mortar; pour the paste into 100cc. of boiling water in a beaker. The starch granules are insoluble but heat ruptures the walls of the granules freeing the contents which dissolve. The cell walls remain in suspension in the liquid and thus give an opalescent solution. Save this starch solution for the tests.

2.—To 5cc. of cold starch solution in a test-tube add a drop of iodine solution and mix well. What is the resulting color? This color is characteristic of starch and iodine solution. It is due to the formation of an iodide of starch, an unstable compound easily decomposed by heat. Heat and observe the effect.

3.—Test 5cc. of the starch solution with Fehling's solution.

4.—Mix 20cc. of the starch solution and 5cc. of dilute hydrochloric acid in a beaker and boil gently, over a low flame, for half an hour; cool and neutralize with sodium hydroxide. Make Fehling's test with a portion of the solution.

5.—To 2g. of starch in an evaporating dish add 1 drop of concentrated nitric acid; heat on a sand bath, stirring constantly, until the mixture becomes light brown in color. When this occurs, remove from flame and dissolve a portion of the mixture in a small amount of water; filter into a test-tube and add a drop of iodine solution. The color is due to dextrin. It varies from purplish to mahogany red depending upon how far the dextrinization has proceeded.

6.—Toast a small piece of bread on wire gauze over a low flame. When well browned, grind up with water in a mortar, filter and test the filtrate with a drop of iodine solution. Does the toast solution give the dextrin reaction?

7.—Study the starch granules of potato, corn, rice, sago, bean, and arrow-root under the low and high power of the microscope. Prepare the slides as follows; Grind a little of the substance with a little water in a mortar; with a glass rod take up one drop of the watery mixture and spread evenly on a glass slide; cover with cover glass and examine. Make drawings of the different granules as they appear under the microscope.

Questions.

1.—What is the difference between the starch used for food and that which is used for laundry purposes?

2.—How could you prepare a soluble starch for laundry use, i. e., a starch which will dissolve in cold water?

3.—Which would be most easily digested, potato or rice starch?

4.—Why is arrow-root starch recommended for invalids' dietaries?

5.—Why is the part of the baked potato next the skin sweeter than the rest?

6.—What digestive value has "zwieback?"

Glycogen. Glycogen, animal starch, is the form in which carbohydrates are stored in the body. It is found principally in the liver and muscle cells. It constitutes a reserve food supply which may be used for the liberation of heat and energy. Before glycogen can be used by the body it must be converted into a soluble form, glucose. This is accomplished by means of a diastase found in the cells of the liver and muscles. Glycogen also occurs in some of the fungi, i. e., plants without chlorophyll, such as yeast.

Glycogen, like ordinary starch, yields glucose when boiled with acids. With iodine solution glycogen gives a port wine coloration. The constitution of glycogen is probably much less complex than that of ordinary starch.

Experiment No. 21.—Glycogen

Reading.—P. & K. p. 564.

   N. p. 374.

   Sherman, pp. 14-16.

Apparatus. Casserole (500cc.), ring-stand, burner, water-bath, 2 beakers, 3 test-tubes.

Material. Fresh liver, alcohol, iodine solution, Fehling's solution, dilute hydrochloric acid, muslin cloth.

Extraction. Add 50 g. of minced liver to a casserole, or large beaker, and cover with 200cc. of water; boil for 20 minutes, then strain through muslin and filter. Concentrate the filtrate on the water bath to about 50cc., cool, and precipitate the glycogen by the addition of 100cc. of alcohol. When the glycogen has settled out, filter and wash the precipitate with a little alcohol. Dissolve the precipitate in water and use this solution for the tests.

Tests.

1.—Make Fehling's test with 5cc. of the solution. Is there any reduction?

2.—Boil about 5cc. of the solution with a few drops of dilute hydrochloric acid for a few minutes; cool, neutralize with sodium hydroxide, and make Fehling's test.

3.—Add a drop of iodine solution to some of the glycogen solution. The color is due to the compound formed by the iodine and glycogen.

Questions.

1.—Why is glycogen called animal starch? Do vegetable cells ever contain glycogen?

2.—What is the function of glycogen in the body?

3.—Which foods yield glycogen in the body?

4.—In the laboratory experiment why must fresh liver be used?

CHAPTER XIII

Pectin

Pectin. Pectin is the substance in fruits and vegetables which gives them their jelly forming properties. It exists in considerable quantity in most ripe fruits and in many vegetables. Apples, plums, currants, grapes and other fruits, as well as carrots and potatoes contain a large amount of pectin. The pectin is generally in the juice and pulp of the food but in some instances it is found in the skin. Miss Goldthwaite* claims that in oranges and lemons the pectin is in the white inner skin lining the peel.

Pectin swells up and dissolves in water forming a viscid liquid which tends to gelatinize when its solutions become at all concentrated. The object in jelly making is to prepare a liquid of such concentration that this gelatinization will occur. The factors influencing the gelatinization are the amount of water, the amount of sugar, and the amount of acid in the fruit juice. When the fruit juices are boiled a considerable amount of water is evaporated off. In making jelly then the solution must be boiled until the right concentration is obtained. This is determined by the ''jell'' test, i. e. allowing the solution to boil until it jells when dropped from a spoon. The amount of sugar added to the fruit juice in making jelly must be proportional to the amount of pectin in the juice. Miss Goldthwaite* gives a method for determining this proportion. The fruit juice must have a certain amount of acid in order to make a good jelly. Frequently jelly is made from non acid fruits by mixing these with acid fruits.

---

*See Bulletin, Principles of Jelly Making by N. E. Goldthwaite, published by the Dept. of Household Science, The University of Illinois.

Experiment No. 22.—Pectin

Reading.—Bul. Dept. of Household Science, University of Illinois—Principles of Jelly-making.—Goldthwaite.

Apparatus. Mortar, 4 beakers, 4 test-tubes, 2 watch glasses.

Material. Apple, carrot, alcohol, sugar, cheese cloth.

Extraction. Cut an apple into small pieces and grind up in a mortar; place pulp in a beaker and add just enough water to cover; boil gently for 10 minutes; strain through 4 thicknesses of cheese cloth. Save juice for tests.

Prepare some carrot juice by treating a carrot in the same way. Make the tests given below, first with the apple juice and then with the carrot juice.

Tests.

1.—Allow 3cc. of the juice to stand in a test-tube for an hour. Does the juice gelatinize on standing?

2.—Add a few drops of alcohol to a little of the juice in a test-tube. The precipitate contains the pectin which is insoluble in alcohol.

3.—Weigh the remainder of the juice, add three-fourths the weight of sugar and boil gently from three to five minutes. Gauge the time by the concentration of the solution. After boiling pour the liquid on a watch glass and allow to cool. Do you get the formation of jelly in each case?

Questions.

1.—Why is fruit juice boiled in making jelly?

2.—Can jelly be made from un-cooked fruits?

3.—In making jelly is there any danger of boiling the fruit juice too long?

4.—Why is sugar used in making jelly?

5.—How could you make orange or lemon jelly?

6.—If a fruit contains too little pectin for jelly formation, how may this be corrected?

CHAPTER XIV

Cellulose

Cellulose. Cellulose, $(C_6H_{10}O_5)n$, is the principal ingredient of the cell membranes of all plants. It is the most complex carbohydrate. It is obtained from plant fiber by treating successively with dilute potassium hydroxide, dilute hydrochloric acid, water, alcohol, and ether, to remove all incrusting substances.

Cellulose is insoluble in all the usual solvents. It dissolves in ammoniacal copper solution, (Schweitzer's reagent), from which solution it may be precipitated with acids.

Cellulose swells up in concentrated sulphuric acid and dissolves forming dextrin. When this solution is diluted and boiled, glucose is formed. Cold concentrated nitric acid, or a mixture of nitric and sulphuric acids, converts cellulose into **nitro-celluloses**, which are used in the preparation of **artifical silk, celluloid, collodion,** and **gun cotton.**

Vegetable parchment is formed when unsized filter paper is treated with dilute sulphuric acid. This is largely used as a substitute for ordinary parchment.

Experiment No. 23.—Cellulose

Reading.—P. & K. pp. 281-283.
        N. pp. 371-372.

Apparatus. Beaker, glass rod, wire gauze, ring-stand, burner, glass slide, microscope, 3 evaporating dishes.

Material. Cotton wool, concentrated sulphuric acid, concentrated sodium hydroxide, Fehling's solution, good grade filter paper, linen.

Tests.

1.—Dissolve 1g. of cotton wool in 5cc. of concentrated sulphuric acid in a beaker, stirring well during the operation.   When the mass becomes semi-liquid, carefully add 15cc. of water and boil on a wire gauze over a low flame for 20 minutes.   Replace the water lost by evaporation.   After boiling, cool the solution, neutralize with concentrated sodium hydroxide solution, and make Fehling's test.   By this treatment cellulose is partly converted into dextrin and glucose.

2.—The best grades of washed filter paper consist of cellulose which is practically pure.   Separate a few fibers from some good grade filter paper and examine on a slide under the microscope.   Make a drawing of the fibers as they appear under the microscope.

3.—Examine some linen fibers under the microscope and compare with the fibers seen in test 2.

4.—Prepare 3 evaporating dishes containing respectively concentrated sulphuric acid, water, and ammonium hydroxide solution.   Dip a piece of unsized paper in the acid bath for an instant and then pass the strip rapidly through the water and the ammonia baths.   Allow the strip to dry; compare its strength with that of some paper which has not been so treated.

CHAPTER XV.—Proteins

Classification

The classification of proteins which the committee on protein nomenclature recommend may be found in many text books.*. A tabulated list of the proteins which occur most commonly in our chief protein foods, i. e., milk, eggs, meat, and vegetables, is given below.

	Protein	Solubility	Occurrence
Simple Proteins	Albumins	sol. in water	albumins of egg, milk, meat
	Globulins	sol. in dilute salt solution and in dilute alkalies	globulins of egg, blood, meat, edestin of wheat
	Glutelins	sol. in dilute acid and alkalies	glutelin of flour
	Alcohol, sol. proteins		gliadin of flour, zein of corn
	Albuminoids	insol. in all neutral solvents	collagen of bone, keratin of skin, elastin of tissues, gelatin, fibroin of silk
Conjugated Proteins	Phosphoproteins	sol. in dilute alkalies	casein of milk, vitellin of egg yolk, legumins of peas and beans
	Nucleoproteins	sol. in alkalies	cell nucleus of plant and animal cells
	Hemoglobin	insol. in water	hemoglobins of blood

*Sherman, Chemistry of Food and Nutrition, pp. 26-29

	Protein	Solubility	Occurrence
Derived Proteins	Coagulated proteins		insol. products resulting from the action of heat or alcohol on proteins
	Proteoses		sol. in water but ppt'd by saturation with ammonium sulphate, derived from proteins by hydrolysis
	Peptones		sol. in water, not ppt'd by saturation with ammonium sulphate— formed by digestion or hydrolysis of proteins

Proteins are the chief constitutents of living protoplasm. They are formed exclusively in plant cells. They consist of carbon, hydrogen, oxygen, nitrogen and sulphur, and some contain phosphorus also. The proteins are very complex compounds and have a high molecular weight. They are built up of anhydrides of the amido acids.

The proteins differ greatly in solubility. With the exception of albumins they are generally insoluble in water. They are also insoluble in alcohol and ether. Most of them are precipitated by mineral acids, by alkalies, by salts of the heavy metals, and by alkaloids. Many proteins are coagulated by heat.

When proteins are hydrolized they yield a large number of products, chief of which are the amido acids. Some of the prominent amido acids formed by protein decomposition are glycin, CH_2NH_2COOH, alanin, CH_3CHNH_2COOH, leucin, $(CH_3)_2CH.CH_2CHNH_2COOH$ and tyrosin, $C_6H_4(OH)CH_2CHNH_2COOH$. The amido acids all contain one or more amido, NH_2, group.

The proteins give certain characteristic color reactions with particular reagents. These color reactions are used in their identification.

Experiment No. 24.—Proteins

Reading—P. & K. pp. 610-614.
N. pp. 509-516.
Sherman, pp. 23-40.

Apparatus. 4 beakers, 2 flasks, 10 test-tubes, 2 evaporating dishes, thermometer, ring-stand, burner.

Material. Egg white, ammonium sulphate, sodium chloride, alcohol, concentrated acids, concentrated alkalies, solutions of mercuric chloride, silver nitrate, lead acetate, copper sulphate, tannic acid, picric acid, ammonium hydroxide, Millon's reagent, milk, gelatine, peptone, litmus solution.

I. Tests With Egg Albumin.

Place the white of an egg in an evaporating dish and cut fine with a pair of scissors; reserve a portion of the white for the tests which call for undiluted egg white; divide the rest of the egg white into two parts and dilute one part with water so as to form a 2 per cent solution; dilute the other portion so as to form a 5 per cent solution. Use the more dilute solution for all tests except these which call for the 5 per cent solution.

1.—**Coagulation.** (a). Place 5cc. of the albumin solution in a test-tube and heat. Notice the coagulation. Repeat this test, first acidifing with a few drops of acetic acid.

(b). Fit a ' test-tube with a perforated cork into which a thermometer has been inserted and fill the test-tube one third full of undiluted egg white. Suspend the tube in a beaker of water and heat gradually, stirring the water during the process. Note the temperature at which cloudiness occurs. Note the temperature at which a solid clot forms.

2.—**Precipitation.** (a). To 5cc. of the albumin solution add a few drops of concentrated hydrochloric acid. What occurs? Try the effect of strong nitric, sulphuric and acetic acids.

(b). Add a few drops of strong sodium

hydroxide to a few cc. of the albumin solution. Repeat the test with strong potassium hydroxide.

(c). Prepare four test-tubes each containing about 4cc. of the egg albumin solution. To the first add a solution of mercuric chloride, drop by drop, until an excess of the reagent has been added. Note the changes which occur. Repeat the experiment with lead acetate solution, silver nitrate solution and a solution of copper sulphate.

(d). To 5cc. of the albumin solution add picric acid, drop by drop until an excess of the reagent has been added. Repeat the experiment with a solution of tannic acid.

(e). Add a few drops of alcohol to 5cc. of the albumin solution. What is the effect?

3.—**Color Reactions.**

(a). **Biuret Reaction.**—To 5cc. of the albumin solution in a test-tube add an equal volume of sodium hydroxide and then add a drop or two of **very dilute** copper sulphate solution. A violet color appears.

(b). **Millon's Reaction.**—Add a few drops of Millon's reagent* to 5cc. of the albumin solution in a test-tube. A precipitate appears which turns reddish on boiling.

(c). **Xanthoproteic Reaction.**—To 5cc. of the albumin solution add an equal volume of concentrated nitric acid. Heat until a yellow precipitate or solution is obtained. Cool thoroughly and then neutralize with concentrated ammonium hydroxide solution. The color changes to orange which is the **X**anthoproteic reaction.

4. **Salting Out Experiments.** (a).—**T**o 25cc. of 5 per cent egg albumin solution in a beaker add **solid** pow-

---

*Millon's reagent is made by dissolving mercury in its own weight of concentrated nitric acid; then adding to the solution twice its volume of water. After standing for a short time the clear liquid is decanted off and used as the reagent.

dered ammonium sulphate to the point of saturation. Keep in the water-bath at about 35° for half an hour. Filter, test the filtrate by the biuret test and the precipitate by Millon's test. When making the biuret test in the presence of ammonium sulphate or magnesium sulphate it is necessary to add an excess of sodium hydroxide, preferably a solid stick. Does the filtrate contain protein? What are your conclusions?

(b). Repeat the above experiment making **the** saturation with solid sodium chloride. How does the result differ from the result of the saturation with ammonium sulphate? All proteins are precipitated from their solutions by saturation with ammonium sulphate **with the exception of the peptones.. Globulins** are the only proteins precipitated by saturation with salt. Can you explain why the water solution of white of egg contains globulins as well as albumins? Are globulins soluble in pure water?

5. **Acid-A**lbuminate.—To 25cc. of egg albumin solution add 2cc. of 0.2 per cent hydrochloric acid and heat on the water-bath at 40° for a few minutes. Acid albumin is formed.

(a). To 5cc. of the solution of acid albumin add a few drops of litmus. The solution becomes red. Now add dilute sodium hydroxide until the solution just changes to blue. The acid albumin is precipitated. It redissolves on the addition of an excess of the alkali.

(b). Heat a portion of the acid albumin solution to boiling. Is a precipitate formed?

6. **Alkali-Albuminate.**—To 25cc. of albumin solution add 5cc. of sodium hydroxide and heat gently for **a** few minutes. Alkali-albuminate is formed whenever albumins or globulins are treated with alkalies.

(a). Add a few drops of litmus to 5cc. of the alkali-albumin solution and just neutralize with dilute hydrochloric acid. What is the precipitate?

(b). Heat a portion of the alkali-albumin solution to boiling and note presence or absence of a precipitate.

II. Tests With Proteins of Milk.

Mix 25cc. of milk with 75cc. of water, warm to 37°, and add dilute acetic acid, drop by drop, stirring, until the casein separates out as a flaky precipitate. Filter and use the precipitate for the tests. Test a portion of the filtrate with biuret and Millon tests.

1.—Test the solubility of the precipitated casein in dilute acids, dilute alkalies, and in water.

2.—Make the biuret and Millon tests with portions of the casein solution.

III. Proteoses and Peptones.

Dissolve 20g. of commercial peptone in 100cc. of water. Warm in order to obtain a complete solution.

1.—Put 5cc. of the solution in a test-tube and heat to boiling. Is there any coagulation?

2.—Make the biuret test with about 5cc. of the solution. What is the color?

3.—To 50cc. of the solution add 50cc. of a saturated ammonium sulphate solution. Stir well. The precipitate consists of the primary albumoses. Filter. To the filtrate add two drops of sulphuric acid and then add solid ammonium sulphate until the solution is saturated. Notice the sticky precipitate that adheres to the stirring rod and to the sides of the beaker. The precipitate consists of the secondary albumoses. Filter; transfer some of the precipitate to a test-tube, dissolve in a little water and make the biuret test. Test a portion of the filtrate for peptone by adding an excess of solid sodium hydroxide and then making the biuret test. Which class of proteins are not precipitated by saturation with ammonium sulphate?

IV. Gelatin.

1.—Test the solubility of some commercial gelatine in cold and hot water, in 0.5 per cent sodium carbonate solution, in 2 per cent hydrochloric acid, in alcohol, in concentrated hydrochloric acid and in concentrated potassium hydroxide solution.

2.—Hydrate 1g. of gelatin with 5cc. of cold water and dissolve by adding 45cc. of boiling water. With portions of this solution make the following tests:

(a) Precipitation. Test with concentrated sulphuric acid, with alcohol, tannic acid, and mercuric chloride.

(b) Color tests. Make biuret, Millon's, and Xanthoproteic tests.

Questions.

1.—Name some of the most common protein foods. Which proteins occur most frequently in our foods?

2.—What is the composition of proteins?

3.—At what temperature should eggs be cooked?

4.—Why is white of egg given in cases of lead or mercury poisoning?

5.—What would be the effect of strong tea on a solution of proteins? Tea contains a considerable amount of tannin.

6.—Why does milk curdle when it sours?

Tabulate the Results of the Protein Experiments According to Following Table:

| PROTEIN | HEAT | PRECIPITANTS | | | | | COLOR REACTIONS | | |
	coagulation	acids	alkalies	salts of heavy metals	alkaloidal reagents	NaCl or $(NH_4)_2 SO_4$	biuret	Millon	Xanthoproteic
Albumin									
Globulin									
Casein									
Proteoses									
Peptones									
Gelatin									

Experiment No. 25.—Tests for nutrients in foods

Reading.—Sherman, pp. 41-44.
        Snyder, pp. 1-27.

With the following foods make tests according to the general scheme* given below:

(a) Bean soup.
(b) Bouillon.
(c) Milk, or commercial ice cream, or any other liquid food.

Scheme for the detection of the more common nutrients.

1.—Preliminary tests.

(a) Test reaction with litmus paper.
(b) Make **X**anthoproteic or biuret tests for proteins. If proteins are present proceed with tests given under 2. If no proteins are indicated proceed with the tests given under 3.

2.—Test for proteins.

(a) **Albuminates.** If the original solution is acid or alkaline: neutralize with dilute sodium carbonate, if acid, or with very dilute sulphuric acid if alkaline. A precipitate in either case indicates the presence of an acid or alkali-albuminate. If the original solution is neutral there are no albuminates in the solution.

(b) **Albumins and globulins.** If the original solution is neutral, acidulate with a few drops of dilute acetic acid and boil. **A** precipitate indicates albumins or globulins. Filter and keep the filtrate for (c). If no precipitate is obtained proceed at once to (c). If a precipitate is obtained saturate some of the original solution with salt. **A** precipitate indicates globulin.

(c) Add to some of the original solution, or to the filtrate from (b), its own volume of saturated ammonium sulphate solution. **A** precipitate indicates primary proteoses. Filter.

(d) Saturate the filter from (c) with solid am-

---

*Stewart, Manual of Physiology, pp. 4-10.

monium sulphate. A precipitate indicates the secondary proteoses. Filter.

(e) Add a stick of solid sodium hydroxide to the filtrate from (d) and make the biuret test. **A** positive reaction indicates peptones.

3.—Test for carbohydrates.

If original solution is opalescent starch or glycogen are indicated.

If original solution contains proteins acidulate with dilute acetic acid and boil, then filter. Use filtrate for tests.

(a) **Starch, glycogen or dextrin.** To a few cc. of the solution add a drop of iodine solution. If solution is alkaline neutralize before adding the iodine solution. **A** blue color indicates the presence of starch. A reddish brown color indicates dextrin or glycogen. Glycogen gives an opalescent solution while dextrin does not.

(b) **Reducing sugar.** Make Fehling's test with a portion of the solution.

(c) **Cane-sugar.** If tests (a) and (b) are negative boil 20cc. of the solution with 1cc. of concentrated hydrochloric acid for a few minutes: neutralize and make Fehling's test. A positive test indicates that cane sugar is present in the original solution.

Tabulate your results as follows:

FOOD	PROTEINS			CARBOHYDRA				
	albumin or globulin	proteose	peptone	starch	dextrin	glycogen	reducing sugar	
....	....	....	....	... .	... .	....	....	....
....	....	....	....	....	....	....	....	....
....	....	....	....	....	....	....	....	....
....	....	....	....	....	....	....	....	....

CHAPTER XVI

Baking Powders

Baking Powders. The value of a baking powder is determined by the amount of available carbon dioxide which it yields and by the character of the residue left in the bread. The first factor is largely influenced by the age of the powder. Even if baking powders are kept closely covered there is considerable loss of carbon dioxide on. standing. The character of the residue depends upon the kind of powder used. Baking powders consist of soda, (sodium bi-carbonate), and an acid salt, mixed with a certain amount of air-dried starch. The starch is hygroscopic and prevents the other substances from becoming moist. The powders are named according to the acid ingredient which they contain. The principal powders are cream of tartar, acid phosphate, and alum powders. The alum powders generally contain some other acid ingredient besides the alum. Alum baking powders are quite generally condemned. The employment of alum in the preparation of any food is considered an adulteration.

The chemical reaction of baking powders is a reaction between the soda and the acid constituent and results in the formation of a sodium salt of the acid and water and carbon dioxide. The salt formed in each case is left as a residue in the bread. The residue from the different powders is shown by the following reactions:

Cream of Tartar Powder

potassium bi-tartrate	sodium bi-carbonate	potassium sodium tartrate
(cream of tartar)	(soda)	(Rochelle salts)

$$KHC_4H_4O_6 + NaHCO_3 \longrightarrow KNaC_4H_4O_6 + CO_2 + H_2O$$

Phosphate Powder

calcium   soda   calcium sodium
acid phosphate   tri hydrogen
                     phosphate

$$CaH_4(PO_4)_2 \; + \; NaHCO_3 \; \rightarrow CaNaH_3(PO_4)_2 + CO_2 + H_2O$$

Alum Powders

potash alum   soda   potassium   sodium
                        sulphate   sulphate

$$Al_2K_2(SO_4)_4.24H_2O + 6NaH\,CO_3 \rightarrow K_2SO_4 \; + \; 3Na_2SO_4$$

aluminum hydroxide   carbon dioxide   water

$$+ \; 3\,Al(OH)_3 \quad + \quad 6CO_2 \quad + \quad 24H_2O$$

The residues from the cream of tartar and phosphate powders are substances used as drugs. Both Rochelle salts and calcium sodium acid phosphate are considered harmless when taken in the small amounts used in leavening agents. The aluminum hydroxide formed as a residue in alum powders is regarded as decidedly deleterious. The continued use of alum powders is said to impair digestion and result in gastric disorders. *

Experiment No. 26.—Baking Powders

Reading.—Leach pp. 332-346.
           Snyder, pp. 186-193.

Apparatus. 5 beakers, 5 evaporating dishes, flask, 10 test-tubes, water-bath, burner, Knorr or Geissler Apparatus for CO_2.

Material. Royal, Rumford, Calumet, K. C., and Unrivalled Baking Powders, dilute hydrochloric acid, barium chloride solution, dilute nitric acid, ammonium molybdate solution, tincture of logwood, ammonium carbonate solution, ammoniacal silver nitrate solution, lime water, resorcin, concentrated sulphuric acid.

---

*Jago—Technology of bread making, p. 467.

Tests.

1.—**Starch.**—Place two grams of the baking powder in a beaker and add 100cc. of water. Heat to boiling and observe the thickness of the starch paste. Make this test with all the powders and compare the different powders in regard to the relative amount of starch which they contain.

Mix 5 grams of the baking powder with 100cc. of distilled water in a flask. Shake well and allow the starch to settle out. Decant the liquid through a filter. Use this solution for the tests given below.

2.—**Sulphates.**—To about 5cc. of the baking powder solution add a few drops of dilute hydrochloric acid and then add 1cc. of barium chloride solution. The formation of a white precipitate, (barium sulphate), indicates the presence of sulphates.

3.—**Phosphates.**—Add a few drops of nitric acid to 5cc. of the baking powder solution and then add 5cc. of ammonium molybdate. The formation of a fine yellow precipitate, especially on warming, indicates the presence of phosphates.

4.—**Tartrates.**—If the baking powder contains phosphates make test (a) for tartrates, otherwise test according to (b).

(a). **Applicable in the presence of** phosphates.

Evaporate 25cc. of the solution to dryness on the water-bath. Transfer the residue to a test-tube, add an equal amount of dry resorcin, and then a few drops of concentrated sulphuric acid. Heat gently. A rose-red color indicates the presence of tartrates.

(b). To 5cc. of the baking powder solution add 2cc. of ammoniacal silver nitrate and warm gently. The formation of a silver mirror on the sides and bottom of the test-tube indicates the presence of tartrates.

5.—**Alum.**—Mix 2 grams of baking powder with 5cc. of water in an evaporating dish; add a few drops of tincture of logwood and 2cc. of ammonium carbonate solution. Heat over water-bath and observe color. **A** blue color indicates alum but a lavender or pink color shows pretty definitely that there is no alum present.

6.—**Available carbon dioxide gas.**—Determine the amount of available carbon dioxide gas in a sample of the baking powder according to the official methods of the Department of Agriculture, Bul. No. 107, Bur. of Chem., pp. 169-175, or, Leach pp. 336-8.

Questions.

1.—Compare prices of pure tartrate and pure phosphate baking powders. Why should an alum powder not be used?

2.—Would it be practical to prepare your own baking powder for use in the home?

The formulas below have been worked out for the preparation of baking powders. Obtain prices of the materials and calculate the amount which could be saved by preparing the powders at home.

Cream of tartar powder	Phosphate powder
cream of tartar ......1lb.	acid phosphate of lime 1¾lb.
baking soda ....½lb.	baking soda ....1lb.
corn starch ....½lb.	corn starch ....1lb.

3.—A baking powder is judged by the amount of available carbon dioxide gas which it yields and by the nature of the residue which it leaves in the bread. If a phosphate and a cream of tartar powder yield the same amount of available carbon dioxide which would you consider best to use?

CHAPTER XVII

Food Adulterants

Foods are adulterated chiefly by the use of substituted products, and by the addition of coloring matter and preservatives.

Food Substitutions. When food materials have been replaced by some inferior or imitation product, the consumer is forced to pay for a direct fraud. Many of the low grade flavoring extracts and so-called cheap teas and coffees consist wholly, or in large part of substituted materials. All substances sold in bulk give the producer a good opportunity for sophistications. Ground spices, mustards, and peppers are frequently badly adulterated. The house-wife may learn to recognize adulterations in this class of products by buying the whole berries and comparing with the suspected articles. It is well to avoid substances sold in bulk not only for economical but for sanitary reasons also.

In some instances food substances command such a high market price that many consumers are forced to use a substituted food. If the substituted food is pure and wholesome and is sold as a substitution, there can be no objection to its use. The use of such foods should be encouraged rather than restricted. The use of substituted vegetable fats in place of the more expensive animal fats is an indication of the desire on the part of the consumer to secure a wholesome product at lower cost. The only danger connected with the sale of butter and lard substitutes is that some unscruplous dealer may sell the artificial for the real article. There are some simple tests, however, which enable the housewife to distinguish between the food and its substitution.

Coloring Matter. The addition of coloring matter to foods may enhance their esthetic appearance but generally such addition serves merely to disguise an inferior artiele. By the use of coloring matter manufacturers of food products are able to palm off on the unsuspecting public inferior, damaged, or substituted materials. Excellent? strawberry preserves are made out of glucose, saccharine, timothy seeds, apple pulp, artificial strawberry flavor, and coloring matter. Without the use of the coloring matter it would be impossible to deceive the consumer. Inferior vinegars are colored to represent the best grade of cider vinegars. Raspberry and other fruit jellies are prepared without a particle of the fruit in them. Tomato refuse is mixed with some cheap pulp, spices are added and then the mixture is colored and put on the market as tomato catsup made from "fresh ripe tomatoes".

The Pure Foods Laws require the use of coloring matter in food products to be stated on the label under which the food is sold. Thus the consumer, if he reads the label, will know he is buying a dyed product.

In testing for coloring matter in foods, it is necessary to distinguish between the artificial coloring matter which has been added to the food, and the natural coloring matter which would be present in the food from fruits or vegetables used in its manufacture. Artificial colors are generally prepared from coal tar products and are called coal tar dyes.

Preservatives. The preservatives most commonly used in foods are formaldehyde, borax and boric acid, sulphites, salicylic acid and sodium salicylate, and benzoic acid and sodium benzoate. Preservatives have much the same effect as coloring matter. By their use damaged, inferior, and spoiled products may be foisted on the public. The addition of a small amount of sodium sulphite to tainted meat restores the fresh red color of the meat and wholly disguises all odors of putridity. If the consumer is deprived of the two ways by which he judges freshness of food products, namely, appearance and odor, he will have little to guide him in the selection of food.

Experiment No. 27.—Tests for some common adulterants in foods

I. **Tests for Formaldehyde in Milk or Cream.**
Leach p. 180.

Apparatus. Test-tube, thistle-tube, porcelain casserole burner.

Material. Milk or cream, concentrated sulphuric acid, concentrated hydrochloric acid (commercial, sp. gr. 1.2,), 10 per cent ferric chloride.

Hehner's Test.—Place 5cc. of milk in a test-tube and add 3cc. of concentrated sulphuric acid through a thistle tube in such a way as to form a distinct layer in the bottom of the tube. The formation of a violet or blue ring at the junction of the two liquids indicates the presence of formaldehyde.

Hydrochloric Acid Test.—Place 10cc. of milk in a porcelain casserole and add an equal volume of concentrated hydrochloric acid to which has been added one drop of 10 per cent ferric chloride. Heat slowly over a small flame for a few moments, giving the casserole a rotary movement to break up the curd. Do not allow the liquid to boil. The presence of formaldehyde is indicated by a violet coloration. This is a very delicate test as it serves to indicate as small an amount of formaldehyde as one part in 250,000 parts of milk.

II. **Tests for Oleomargarine and Process Butter.**

Apparatus. Table spoon, burner, splint of wood, beaker, pan.

Material. Butter, oleomargarine, process or renovated butter, milk.

"Spoon Test."..Farmers' Bul. 131.—Place a lump of the sample in a table spoon and heat over a small flame, stirring constantly. Pure butter boils quietly and foams a great deal. Oleomargarine sputters noisily and foams scarcely at all.

Waterhouse Test.

Farmers' Bul. No. 131.—Heat 50cc. of sweet milk in a beaker and when near boiling add 5 grams of the fat. Stir with a small splint until the fat is melted. Place beaker in a pan of ice water and continue stirring until the fat solidifies. At this point, if the sample is oleomargarine, the fat can be collected in one lump at the end of the stirrer. Butter can not be so collected but will remain in a granular condition distributed through the milk.

In the "Spoon" test the sample if process butter will behave like oleomargarine, i. e., will not foam. In the Waterhouse test process butter behaves like true butter, that is, it can not be collected by the stirrer.

III. Test for Cotton Seed Oil in Compound Lard, Olive Oil, etc.

Leach p. 518.

Apparatus. Beaker, test-tube, ring-stand, burner.

Material. Lard, olive oil, Halphen's reagent, (equal volumes of amyl alcohol and carbon bisulphide, the latter containing 1 per cent of free sulphur), saturated salt solution, cotton wool, cotton seed oil.

Halphen Test.

Mix 5cc. of the sample with an equal volume of Halphen's reagent in a test-tube; stopper the test-tube loosely with cotton wool, and suspend in a beaker of boiling saturated salt solution. **(Precaution!** Care must be taken to prevent the mixture in the test-tube from catching on fire. Do not use a high flame. Have test-tube suspended in an upright position.) Keep the test-tube in the boiling solution for 15 minutes. If the oil darkens, i. e., shows a red or orange coloration, the presence of cotton seed oil is indicated. Make a control test with cotton seed oil.

IV. Test for Coal-Tar Colors in Ketchup, or Jelly, Jam or Candy.

Leach pp. 907, 794.

Apparatus. 4 beakers, ring-stand, burner.

Material. Sample of ketchup or whatever substance is

to be tested, 10 per cent hydrochloric acid, strips of pure white woolen cloth, 1 per cent hydrochloric acid, 1 per cent sodium hydroxide, 2 per cent ammonium hydroxide.

Method of Sostegni and Carpentieri, Zts. anal. Chem., 1896, 35:397.

Dissolve about 20 grams of the sample in 100cc. of water, filter into a beaker and add 3cc. of 10 per cent hydrochloric acid. Prepare some strips of fat free woolen cloth by washing strips of pure white wool in a 1 per cent solution of sodium hydroxide and then washing well in water to remove the alkali. Immerse a strip of this cloth in the acid solution in the beaker and boil over a low flame for 10 minutes. Remove the cloth to another beaker, cover with 1 per cent hydrochloric acid and boil. Pour off the acid, wash well with water, cover with a 2 per cent solution of ammonium hydroxide and boil again. As soon as the ammonia solution has taken up the color well, remove the cloth and immerse a second strip of fat free wool in the ammonia solution. Acidify the solution with a little dilute hydrochloric acid and boil for a few minutes. Examine the second strip of wool carefully. If it is colored, coal-tar dyes are indicated. Vegetable and fruit colors give no color to the wool in this second dyeing.

V. Test for Copper Salts in Canned Peas, Beans, or in Pickles.

Leach pp. 897-899.

Apparatus. Large evaporating dish (250cc.), ringstand, burner.

Material. Can of peas or other material, concentrated sulphuric acid, concentrated nitric acid, concentrated ammonium hydroxide.

Evaporate the contents of the can to dryness in a large evaporating dish; add to the dry residue 10cc. of concentrated sulphuric acid and heat gently over a low flame until foaming ceases. Then burn the residue to an ash in a hot flame. Moisten the ash with a few drops of concentrated nitric acid, add 50cc. of water, transfer to a beaker and boil; cool, make strongly alkaline with ammonium hydroxide and filter. If the filtrate is colored blue it is an indication that copper salts are present.

VI. Test for Saccharin in Candies, Jellies, Jams, Syrups or Canned Products.

Leach, pp. 842-843.

Apparatus. Beaker, separatory funnel, evaporating dish, water-bath, test-tube.

Material. Sample to be tested, phosphoric acid, ether, resorcin, concentrated sulphuric acid concentrated sodium hydroxide.

Bornstein's Test.

Macerate 50 grams of the sample in a mortar, dissolve in water, and strain through muslin. If filtrate is not already acid, acidify with a few drops of phosphoric acid. Extract with ether in a separatory funnel. Evaporate the ethereal extract to dryness over hot water. **Avoid flame!** Mix the residue in the evaporating dish with an equal amount of dry resorcin and transfer to a test-tube. Add a few drops of concentrated sulphuric acid and heat until the mixture swells up; remove from flame and after the action ceases, heat again; repeat the heating and cooling several times. Finally cool, dilute with water and neutralize with sodium hydroxide. If saccharine is present the solution will show a red-green fluorescence.

VII. Test for Starch and Gelatin in Jellies, Jams, Strained Honey, etc.

Leach, pp. 922, 914, 915.

Apparatus. 2 beakers, 2 test-tubes, ring-stand, burner.

Material. Jelly, dilute sulphuric acid, potassium permanganate, iodine solution, alcohol, tannic acid solution, quicklime, hydrochloric acid, muslin cloth.

Detection of Starch.—Mix 25 grams of the sample with 50cc. of water, stir well, and strain through muslin. Heat the filtrate to boiling, remove from flame and decolorize by the addition of dilute sulphuric acid and potassium permanganate. Filter some of the clarified solution into a test-tube, cool and test for starch by the addition of a drop of iodine solution.

Detection of Gelatine. Make an aqueous extract of 25 grams of the sample, strain through muslin, and add to the filtrate sufficient strong alcohol to precipitate the gelatine. Divide the precipitate into two parts. Dissolve one part in water in a test-tube and add a few drops of tannic acid. A precipitate indicates gelatine.

Transfer the remainder of the precipitate to a test-tube and add a small lump of quicklime. Heat and test the vapors for ammonia gas. Test odor, reaction to moist litmus, and reaction to hydrochloric acid fumes. If gelatine is present ammonia will be given off by treatment with the quicklime.

VIII.   Tests for Chicory and Cereals in Coffee.
Leach, pp. 386, 388, 389.
Snyder, pp. 203-214.

Apparatus.   Hand lens, 2 small flasks.

Material.   Pure roasted coffee beans, low grade coffee, saturated salt solution, chicory.

Pure Coffee.   (a).   Obtain some properly roasted coffee beans of the best grade of coffee. Make a physical examination and also examine with a hand lens.

(b).   Grind up one gram of the pure sample in a mortar; transfer to a small flask and add 25cc. of saturated salt solution. Shake well and then examine. The liquid should be amber colored and nearly all the material should float upon the surface.

Chicory.—Repeat the tests given above with a sample of low grade coffee. Chicory is more soluble than coffee and is also heavier. A cold water extract of coffee which contains chicory will show more color than will pure coffee. In test (b) the formation of much of a sediment indicates the presence of chicory. Make tests (a) and (b) with pure chicory. Compare the taste of chicory with that of coffee.

Cereals.—Examine the low grade coffee with the hand lens for the detection of cereals. Roasted cereals show a polished surface which is very different from that of the roasted coffee bean.

IX.　Tests for Adulterants in Tea.
Leach, pp. 374, 376, 378.

Apparatus.　Casserole, flask, (500cc.), sieve, beaker, hand lens or microscope.

Material.　Samples of high and low grade tea.

Stems and Foreign Leaves.—Boil a gram of tea with 200cc. of water in a casserole for 20 minutes. Pour off the water and examine the leaves. Make this test with tea which is known to be pure and with samples of low grade varieties. The presence of stems, dust, and foreign leaves can be detected in this way.

Facing.—Mix two grams of tea with 500cc. of water in a flask. Shake well and strain through a sieve. Allow the insoluble materials remaining in the water to settle, then filter and examine the sediment for mineral matter. The mineral pigments can readily be seen when the sediment is examined under the microscope.

X.　Tests for Adulterants in Vanilla Extracts.
Leach, pp. 849-855.

Apparatus. Evaporating dish, water-bath, separatory funnel, 2 test-tubes, burner.

Material. High and low grade vanilla extracts, 10 percent ammonium hydroxide, chloroform, iodine solution, (2g. of crystallized potassum iodide dissolved in 100cc. of water and saturated with iodine).

Test for Coumarin (Extract of Tonka Bean.).
Leach, p. 859.

Leach's Test.—Place 35cc. of the extract in an evaporating dish and heat on the water-bath until the alcohol is driven off. Dissolve the residue in 10cc. of 10 per cent ammonium hydroxide and extract with three portions of chloroform in a separatory funnel. Evaporate the chloroform extract to dryness on the water-bath; add 5cc. of water to the residue and warm gently. Filter into a test-tube, cool and add a few drops of iodine solution. If coumarin is present a brown precipitate will form and on stirring this will gather in dark green flakes, leaving a clear brown solution.

Compare samples of pure vanilla extract with extract of tonka. Note the difference in odor and taste.

Artificial Vanilla—Add a few drops of lead acetate to 5cc. of the sample in a test-tube. The absence of a precipitate indicates the artificial product. **A**n extract of the vanilla bean under these conditions forms a copious white precipitate which soon settles to the bottom of the test-tube. A faint cloudiness should not be mistaken for a precipitate.

XI. Test for Oil of Lemon in Lemon Extracts.
Leach, 862, 863, 864.

Oil of Lemon.—To one cc. of the extract in a test-tube add 10cc. of water. The amount of cloudiness indicates the amount of oil of lemon present. If no cloudiness results the oil is absent. Compare samples of low and high grade extracts in this respect.

BIBLIOGRAPHY

Sherman, Chemistry of Food and Nutrition. New York, 1906.*

Snyder, Human Foods. New York, 1908.*

Leach, Food Inspection and Analysis. New York, 1909.*

Snyder, Chemistry of Plant and Animal Life. New York, 1909.

Richter, Organic Chemistry. Phil., 1905.

Mann, Chemistry of the Proteins, London, 1906.

Howell, Text-Book of Physiology, Phil., 1910.

Stewart, Manual of Physiology, Phil., 1905.

Hammarsten, A Text-Book of Physiological Chemistry, Translated by Mandel, New York, 1904.

Hawk, Practical Physiological Chemistry. Phil., 1909.

Bevier and Usher, Food and Nutrition Laboratory Manual, Boston, 1908.

Webster and Koch, A Laboratory Manual in Physiological Chemistry, Chicago, 1903.

Rockwood, A Laboratory Manual in Physiological Chemistry, Phil., 1906.*

Garret and Harden, An Elementary Course in Practical Organic Chemistry, London, 1907.*

Effront, Enzymes and their Applications. (Translated by Prescott), New York, 1902.

Blyth, Foods, their Composition and Analysis, New York, 1903.

Halliburton, A text book of Physiological Chemistry, London, 1891.

Jago, Technology of Bread Making. Am. Edition, Chicago, 1911.*

Salkowski, A Laboratory Manual of Physiological and Pathological Chemistry, (translated by Orndoff), New York, 1904.

Simon, A Text-Book of Physiological Chemistry, New York, 1901.

Thorpe, Outlines of Industrial Chemistry, New York, 1907.

Sadtler, Industrial Organic Chemistry, Phil., 1908.

Knight, Food and its Functions, London, 1895.

Green, The Soluble Ferments and Fermentation, Cambridge, 1901.

Goldthwaite, Principles of Jelly Making, Bul, Dept. of Household Science, Univ. of Illinois.*

Bulletin of the Office of Experiment Station, U. S. Dept. of Agric., Nos. 21, 28, 69. 65, 13, 77, 84, 131, 121, 161, 107, 193.*

www.ingramcontent.com/pod-product-compliance
Lightning Source LLC
LaVergne TN
LVHW010653200726
843507LV00011B/1855